Endless Sea Of Stars

Elizabeth F. Shearly

Also By Elizabeth F. Shearly

ENDLESS SEA
OF STARS

ELIZABETH F. SHEARLY

Content Notes

Sexually explicit scenes, liberal use of obscenities.

See the book's page on Elizabeth F. Shearly's website for detailed content notes. Take care of yourself!

Scan or tap for detailed content notes; contains spoilers!

Chapter 1

Shit. Shit, shit, shit. Jeanie was making a stupid decision. Her hip twinged rhythmically, almost in time with the blaring emergency alarm. She'd never make it all the way back to the hangar, even at a flat-out run, let alone at this pace. Not without doing permanent damage. Why had she thought it was a good idea to store MS1479 locked in the safe? She climbed the final ladder and made it to the gallery. They'd sealed off an old docking bay and kept all their valuables in here, including the fireproof safe. Fireproof, sure, but there was no way it would survive the imminent collapse of their moon.

Jeanie hobbled across the gallery toward the safe, making her way around a hulking decommissioned escape pod they'd bought at auction shortly after establishing their shop on this godforsaken moon. Tinkering with the thing had been her and Liam's only source of entertainment the past few years.

Jeanie tried to pick up the pace and used a display case for support. A pang of nostalgia hit Jeanie: the controls of her first ship lay inside, along with Liam's systems designer designation. Liam had wanted to put their marriage certificate in there as well, but the controls already took up most of the case, and Jeanie had prevailed.

The ground rumbled and shook, catapulting Jeanie into their old spacesuits displayed in a corner, and she landed in a heap on the floor. These old things were heavy, but hers had served her well.

Jeanie crawled the rest of the way to the safe and pressed her palm to the lock, but nothing happened. There was no power. Maybe it was being diverted to the emergency systems? Who the hell designed a safe that you couldn't open in an emergency? Isn't that when everyone wants to get their shit out of it?!

Jeanie searched her tool belt for something to pop the emergency keypad open and grabbed her pry bar. Triggering the break-in alarm on the thing by being too rough with it would only make her job harder. She popped the keypad easily and tapped in her backup code. The click of the safe opening was drowned out by an ear-splitting crack, and a jagged line snaked its way across the ceiling.

Jeanie wrenched open the door of the safe and snatched MS's data-stick. She jammed it into her jumpsuit pocket and hauled herself to her feet. Every lurching step set her blowtorch smacking against her leg until Jeanie couldn't stand it anymore. She unclasped her tool belt and dropped it by the old escape pod, only vaguely aware of the alarm still blaring throughout the base. She took a deep breath. Was she going to stand here and die, or get the fuck off this cursed rock?

"Fucking! Spacer! Jagged! Bastard!" she huffed with each step of her left leg, along with the shot of pain that lanced up through her hip. She had walked much too fast on the way here. How had she ever thought she could make it up here and back to the hangar in time? A sob shook her chest. Typical these days. How the fuck was crying going to help her? She shook her head, trying to get rid of the watery jumble in her vision, but it just made the stupid fucking tears run down her face, and they didn't stop.

Jeanie had made it a few metres down the corridor outside the gallery toward the hangar and their ship—her only way off this moon—when she paused to lean against the wall, panting. She needed to take the weight off her left leg, just for a minute. She tipped her head back. Maybe this was how she died. Trying to save her only friend, MS1479, a friend that she'd built from the ground up, pouring years of her life—of herself—into it, and failing. She wasn't melodramatic enough to think that it would be sweet to die together. MS1479 was an AI, and Jeanie knew that there was no comparison between a living thing and a machine learning algorithm.

Pounding footsteps made her whip her head up.

"Jeanie!" said Liam, running toward her. "Where the fuck have you been?" He sounded angry; he sounded scared. He had been frantically trying to find her while she'd been more concerned with her stupid AI pet. Was this what their marriage had come to? She cared more about a neural net than she did about her husband? He didn't wait for her response, just swept her up in his arms and turned back the way he'd come, toward the hangar.

"My hip," said Jeanie, but she didn't think he heard her. She let herself be carted through the corridor like a sack of patching compound. Liam could pick her up easily, but it probably would have been better if he'd let her hobble along to save his energy. He would never listen if she tried to protest, though, and there was no time for a fight about it.

The ground shook again, and Liam staggered and had to put her down. He shoved her into a doorway and crammed himself inside just as, with an ear-splitting crack and ground-shaking rumble, the corridor ahead of them crumbled and collapsed, choking them with dust.

Jeanie coughed. "Well, shit," she said.

Liam had that look on his face as if he was plotting trajectories in his head. He nodded and made to grab Jeanie's hand without a word.

"What's the plan?" she said, snatching her hand away and crossing her arms over her chest.

"What? We don't have time to discuss it," said Liam.

"You telling me we don't have time to discuss it is wasting our time," said Jeanie, still not moving. He could pick her up and carry her wherever he wanted to go, but she would be damned if she would let him shut her out of this. Their lives depended on the choice they made right now.

"We can get through the maintenance access into the hangar if we—"

"Nope, I can't get through any crawlspaces right now," said Jeanie. She didn't even feel bad for cutting him off. There was no point in pursuing an avenue that she already knew was a dead end. Like this damned corridor.

She turned and started walking back the way they'd come, again. It was the only option, and she was slow enough that every step counted. Liam walked silently beside her, keeping himself on a tight leash.

"You can, though," said Jeanie. She refused to imagine him sprinting away to their ship, leaving her behind to explode here, alone.

Liam *snarled*, making Jeanie startle. She had never heard him make a sound like that before, in the nearly ten years they'd known each other.

"I'll take that as a no," said Jeanie, and she couldn't keep from grimacing. "Determined to die together, are you?"

"I can do this," said Liam. "Just give me a minute."

Jeanie couldn't help noticing that he still wasn't including her in the process. She sighed. She would have to make him.

"We need to get off this rock," she said. It was best to start with the obvious and work from there.

"And we don't have much time," said Liam. That wasn't helpful, so Jeanie ignored him.

"That means we need a ship. Something spaceworthy," said Jeanie.

"But it doesn't need to be able to survive in an atmosphere. Whatever there was on this moon is long gone. There's just going to be plasma and maybe vaporized rock, depending on what caused the instability," said Liam, finally thinking aloud.

"And we need to be able to get to it," said Jeanie. "That means no crawlspaces and something within a few dozen metres. The closer the better."

"We don't even know for sure which passages and corridors are still open. We can't get to our ship, and that rust bucket we finished off this morning is long gone. We've got a few salvages, but they're hardly spaceworthy, and they're in the main bay. Far. Probably inaccessible by now," said Liam.

His movements were jerky with the effort to stay at the slow walking pace Jeanie was setting. She huffed and threw her arm around his shoulders, trying to take some weight off her left leg. It didn't make them go any faster, but it was marginally less painful.

Where could they get to? They were still close to the gallery, but it was just odds and ends, nothing that would help them. The ground shook again, and they staggered across the corridor. Thankfully, nothing collapsed this time.

"See? This is why space stations have fucking escape pods every two feet," Liam grumbled. "Goddamned idiotic moon base."

Jeanie gripped Liam's arm tightly, another surge of adrenalin dulling the pain in her hip.

"The escape pod!" she said.

"What? No, Jeanie, that thing is barely—"

"*Barely*! Exactly! That means it is. Would you rather stay here and die?"

"You think it'll get off the ground?" said Liam.

"Pretty soon there won't be a ground to get off of! *Now* you can carry me," said Jeanie. She didn't have to insist; Liam scooped her up and threw her over his shoulder, running full tilt down the corridor, back toward their gallery, back toward the old broken-down escape pod. Their pet project that could maybe, possibly keep them alive.

Liam put Jeanie down beside the escape pod and nudged her toward the ladder that led up the side to the hatch. She dodged him and swiped her toolstrip off the floor before heading that way. Liam took a quick circuit around the pod. It had been a while since he evaluated it for spaceworthiness. He'd been wrestling with the systems for a couple years; they were honest to god, not in the derogatory way, written in TreeEnt, a language that was so ancient that its creators had pulled the name from a 2D video. He broke into a cold sweat thinking of being sealed in this thing for who knew how long. He took a deep breath to slow his pounding heart. It was their only option.

He spotted their old spacesuits heaped in a corner; they were going to need them. The suits had been replaced eighteen months ago and retired to their little nostalgia room, but they were still fully functional. He used the mag hooks on the suits to lash them together and slung them on his back to free his hands for the climb up the side of the pod.

Maybe he could send Jeanie out in this hunk of junk, get back to the hangar, grab their real ship, and meet her—

The ground gave another shake that almost knocked him loose from the ladder, and the crack snaking its way across the ceiling widened, sprinkling him with shards of polymer. Nope. They were out of time. He launched himself toward the hatch and dove through. He dumped the old spacesuits onto the floor of the airlock and poked his head down into the living space. Jeanie was already sitting in the pilot's seat, doing the preflight check, getting the systems warmed up. He sealed the outer hatch, climbed down through the airlock door, and sealed that behind him, too. He looked over Jeanie's shoulder.

"Strap yourself in," she tossed back at him. For a second, he considered insisting on taking the controls, but Jeanie was a better, more experienced pilot, and she was already there. He crammed himself into the rumble seat and clicked the harness into place.

This escape pod was designed to withstand impact, but only just. The thing would protect the occupants, even at the cost of itself, but it could only do so once. It wouldn't help them escape this place. Liam could just see out the front screen from the rumble seat, and though the crack in the ceiling had reached all the way to the bay doors, they were still sealed. Jeanie was swearing a blue streak, just audible over the rumbling engines vibrating his entire body. Engines? This little thing didn't have damned engines! The ground vibrated the entire ship, making Liam's teeth rattle.

"Why did we permanently seal this bay? What a spacer move!" Jeanie ranted while she pounded the console, trying to find any way of blasting through.

"We can make it," Liam said. "There's a crack opening up around the bay doors. We can punch through."

"Punch through? With what propulsion?" she said.

"Use the blast launcher!" Liam was yelling now, but he didn't care. The launcher was intended to blast off the side of a ship in an emergency, but it was all they had for propulsion.

Jeanie was using every curse word she knew, most of them unfamiliar to Liam. She was a true sailor, one of the things that he loved about her. Liam braced himself for impact as Jeanie did as he suggested and launched the pod, the blast rocketing them off the back wall of the gallery. He jerked at the impact with the doors, but they made it through easily, a testament to how close of a call this had been. Chunks of polymer flew past the porthole across from him.

Liam's ears rang in the dead silence. All he could see outside was stars, even when he leaned forward to look out the front screen. Liam's stomach lurched and his entire body jolted into his seat as the pseudo grav unit kicked in. The hum of the life support system clicking on was reassuring. It was still so fucking quiet. Jeanie panted softly in the pilot's seat. For some reason, he didn't want to break the silence. Another alarm did it for him.

"Fuck," said Jeanie, just sounding tired.

"What?" said Liam. He unbuckled his harness and looked over her shoulder.

"Fuel leak," said Jeanie.

Chapter 2

L iam cursed quietly and headed for the airlock and adjacent maintenance area. He didn't want to think about what would have happened if he hadn't grabbed their old suits from the gallery on his way in. They didn't need the fuel to survive, and they could vent it to the vacuum before it built up and exploded. But if they wanted to arrive somewhere safely, they would need to, at the very least, match velocities to dock or land safely. If they could even find an inhabited station or base, alter their course to get to it—he was getting ahead of himself. *Focus.*

"Where are you going?" said Jeanie, suddenly at his elbow. She was leaning heavily on the back of the pilot's chair.

"To patch the fuel tank," he said, letting his tone add the *obviously* subtext.

"Pretty sure I'm the one who should be doing that," said Jeanie.

Like hell was he going to let her collapse in the maintenance area. "How's your hip?" he said. Jeanie couldn't quite hide her hurt look, but even before he saw it, he knew that he was being nasty, that she was just as frustrated with her chronic injury as he was. But by this point, she could barely stand, let alone squeeze into the maintenance area in a heavy suit and apply the patch. Her face fell, and Liam didn't wait for her answer, just grabbed the patching compound, popped the airlock, threw on his suit, and passed into the maintenance area.

This damned pod. The actuation system was as old as you could get. Fuel cells powering the actuators and minimal thrust capability. Without the blast launcher, this pod wouldn't have made it out of the sealed bay at all. Liam cursed the previous owner of the pod to float in space, perpetually kept alive by a tiny suit for the rest of time. Then immediately took it back. That owner had added a fusion core to the tiny pod, crammed into the maintenance bay, which was already cramped. Liam could barely squeeze in between the fusion core and fuel tanks. That being said, without the steady trickle of power from the fusion core, they'd be dependent on fuel to run the life support system. Fuel that was currently bleeding away every second he stood here.

"The crack is in the H_2 tank," said Jeanie through his communicator, making him jump. She'd already patched the ship's communication to his much more modern suit. The flag she threw up onto his helmet's overlay indicated the location of the crack, and he checked it out. He ran his glove over the faint jagged line. Patching compound would take care of this, no problem. He slit open the pack and scooped a handful out. Liam paused before spreading it on, wishing he had let Jeanie take over. She was the one who had run her own ship for years, had dealt with a hundred emergencies all on her own, and survived them all. Hand that woman a blowtorch and a wrench, and she could fix anything.

He peered at the barely visible crack and slapped on the patching compound. Maybe Jeanie would be better at it, but he would get the job done. And keep them from exploding. A hydrogen leak in a tiny pod like this was a recipe for a fiery death. He smeared the compound over the crack, layer after layer. Liam stood back and surveyed his repair. It wasn't pretty, but the crack was definitely covered.

"Tank pressure at ninety-two point six percent," said Jeanie's steady voice over the comms.

"I missed a spot," said Liam.

"Yup, a small one," said Jeanie.

"Where? I don't have much compound left," said Liam. He tried to find the gap himself, but without any guidance, he could be searching a long time.

"On the underside," said Jeanie's voice in his ear.

He'd have to get down on the floor. And he'd thought he couldn't be wedged in here any tighter. He sighed and started squeezing his suit down to the ground.

"Hang on!" said Jeanie.

Liam didn't even have time to ask what the fuck she was talking about before the pod lurched and threw him against the fusion core. *Pop*! Liam froze. Popping sounds in a sealed environment were never good.

"Fuck," he said. "Actuators malfunctioning or something?"

He carefully picked himself up off the floor, and the slight tickle of air movement at his shoulder made him wince.

"Dammit, your suit just lost pressure," said Jeanie.

"It's fine," said Liam, "the positive pressure in the suit'll keep the H_2 out."

"Fine," snapped Jeanie. "Fix it up and get out of there. Don't waste your suit's air."

Once Liam found the crack, it only took a second to slap on the last of the patching compound; it was just a hairline. He sighed and slid out from under the tank, finally relaxed. He scanned the maintenance area for the fucker that had pierced his suit. One of the bolts on the fusion core no one had bothered to saw flat. The previous owner had really done a number on this pod.

Liam quickly emerged from the maintenance bay, sealed it off, and opened up his suit. They would have to stay out of the bay for a while, but the recycler would get it cleared eventually. Liam pulled his suit the rest of the way off and stashed it, fingering the puncture. It was bigger than he'd thought, and they were out of patching compound. Maybe he could use the printer to make a patch that would work for the time being. Might have to trick it, though. Some of these old food printers went haywire if you tried to print textiles or spare parts. Probably just their luck the one on this rust bucket would fall into that category.

Jeanie waited until the airlock clicked shut behind Liam before calling him every fucking name she could think of. They both knew he'd screw up this patch job. But she still didn't waste any time. If he was going to fix the fuel leak, she'd have to dumb it down for him. It was surprisingly easy to open a comms channel with Liam's suit, probably the more modern tech doing some of the fiddly bits automatically, because the goddamned TreeEnt pod sure wasn't helping.

Finding the crack didn't take long either, and she put a pin in it that Liam's suit could display. It was the actual pressure sensor and diagnostics that were hidden away from the main interface, and Jeanie didn't have a hope of interpreting the ancient code.

She whipped MS out of her pocket and plugged her trusty co-pilot into the console. She waited impatiently to see how MS and the pod would interact, and sure enough, when she tried again to access the diagnostic info, she got results. And the results said that Liam had missed a hairline.

"Tank pressure at ninety-two point six percent," said Jeanie, trying not to sound accusatory.

A point caught her eye on the front screen. It was getting larger, but not moving. The pod should at least be smart enough not to let them collide with anything, especially something that big. She absently tapped through to locate the hairline for Liam.

That was a big rock. And it still wasn't moving in the front screen. That meant they were headed toward it on a collision course. Maybe the old nav system on this thing had a shorter range than the newer ones she was used to.

The nav system might still pick it up if she gave it another minute. Jeanie could manoeuvre manually, but it was risky, especially with Liam unrestrained in the maintenance area. There was still time, but why wasn't the nav system kicking in? Jeanie jumped as a prox alarm went off. The ship knew the rock was there, and it still wasn't turning. Were they out of fuel? She quickly checked the gauge. No, they were down to the very dregs, but there was still enough to make the turn. So why wasn't the ship turning? There was no more time to wait for Liam to finish.

"Hang on," she said over comms and mashed the Manual button. She grabbed the controls and swung them up so their trajectory carried them past the rock, with a few dozen kilometres to spare. Something heavy thumped on the deck above her, and a warning flashed up on the console.

"Fuck," said Liam. "Actuators malfunctioning or something?"

"Dammit, your suit just lost pressure," said Jeanie. There was no reason to worry Liam with the nav malfunction now. He was saying something, but Jeanie barely heard him; she was watching the vitals transmitted from his suit.

"Fine," she said. "Fix it up, and get out of there. Don't waste your suit's air."

Jeanie tried to run a diagnostic on the nav system, but she couldn't wrestle the TreeEnt into submission. She would give MS a few minutes and run the query again. Her old ship had had voice chat functionality with MS, but she doubted the pod's system was capable of that level of sophistication. She'd have to ask Liam whether he could set something up.

Jeanie whipped her chair around and popped the harness open. She unclasped her tool belt and plunked it on the single square of countertop in the galley. It was almost within reach of the pilot's seat, and the maintenance column at the other end of the living deck was almost within arm's reach of that.

Jeanie went to the tiny galley sink and splashed water on her face. The important thing was that all the life support systems were working: air, recycler, food printer, gravity. At least for the time being.

Liam's shoulders were hunched, and his jaw was set when he came through from the airlock. He practically fell into the rumble seat across from Jeanie. She filled him in on the near-collision and that she suspected the nav system was malfunctioning.

"Did you patch your suit?" she asked. It really wasn't safe to travel without a functioning suit for everyone on board. Liam scrubbed his face with his hands before he answered.

"I ran out of patching compound," he said.

What the fuck? Jeanie took a couple of deep breaths. All of their compound on one repair? That pack could have lasted them weeks. It was obvious that they would have a lot more repair work to do on this rust bucket. No point in griping about it now. There was something to be said for marital harmony when they were going to be trapped in this tiny pod for the foreseeable future.

"We'll figure it out," said Jeanie. "Besides, it was my course correction that made you fall."

They locked eyes, and Jeanie caught her breath. She sat there, transfixed for a long moment. Liam stood slowly, holding her gaze.

"How will you make it up to me?" he said softly. Jeanie's heart pounded, her abdomen tightening as he came closer. God it had been so long. It was the adrenalin, she knew it was, but she didn't care. She missed this, she missed their games, and the feel of his body, the way his voice changed when he got into it, the way he looked at her. She stepped toward him and bit back a scream as a shot of pain lanced down her leg. Her fucking hip.

The heat left Liam's eyes, and he caught her as she fell into him.

"Fuck, sorry," he said. "I forgot."

And what the hell did that mean? He was sorry he came on to his own wife? He was sorry he wanted to fuck after they almost died? As if she were incapable of being turned on since she got hurt, as if he were imposing himself on her.

He was just trying to be considerate; he didn't want to hurt her.

"I'll be okay," she said, but Liam shook his head.

"You rest. I'll take a shift here," he said.

"Liam, I'm capable of sitting and watching a console," she said. But the truth was that she was tired, and if she could sleep for a bit, maybe when she woke up her hip would feel less as if it were being pried out of the socket.

"Go, rest. There are some things I want to check anyway," he said and stepped aside so she could pass by him to the lower deck.

Her front brushed against his as she went by, and she caught his familiar scent and paused. His arms wrapped around her, and she leaned into his chest and listened to his steady heartbeat. It felt so good to just be here in his arms. It felt so safe, even though she knew intellectually that his arms wouldn't protect her from the vacuum of space or an exploding moon. He dropped a kiss on the top of her head, let her go, and scooched by.

"Go, Jeanie," he said, sat in the pilot's chair, and turned away from her.

Jeanie thought it would take her a long time to fall asleep, but once she hobbled down to the cabins and lay on a bunk, she barely had time to worry about Liam dismissing her so easily before she was sound asleep.

Liam took a deep breath and tried to let the tension ebb from his body. *Great time to think with your dick, asshole.* Behind him, Jeanie clattered down the steep steps to the cabins and then silence. He had only partially been telling the truth: he did want her to rest, but also he needed to get away from her, to cool his head. Sometimes he forgot that she was so fragile, especially after the day they had had. Seeing her hobbling down those corridors was one of the worst experiences of his life, especially knowing that it was his fault that she had gotten hurt in the first place.

Liam started the diagnostics for the clearly nonfunctional nav system with a few commands. What the hell had Jeanie been thinking, letting them get so close to that rock? Every guideline stated that safe distance was, what, a hundred times the distance she'd left? He smiled in spite of himself. Jeanie's recklessness was part of who she was, part of what had drawn him to her. She always pushed the limits, but she always came through unscathed in the end. Maybe he needed to trust her a little more, but maybe she needed to be a little more cautious as well, especially when both their lives hung in the balance.

The grumpy console beeped, and Liam checked it out. Of course, the fucking TreeEnt code structure didn't have universal diagnostics embedded, which meant he had to go through every single system component manually and test them all. He and Jeanie had both fallen in love with this pod at one point. There were so many oddities to explore, so many questions surrounding the modifications and the relics it contained. It wasn't something they had ever thought their lives would depend on. If he'd known this was going to happen, he would have ripped the entire system out and replaced it with an up-dated control scheme, and he was sure Jeanie would have torn all the wiring out of the pod and redone it from scratch as well. Plus the core. And the hull. And *that's* why they had a different ship.

After a series of seemingly interminable tests and beeps, the console finally flashed a useful message. There was a problem with the power supply to the nav system, something about it cutting out or flickering? Maybe the wiring was frayed or broken, or maybe the system just needed a reset to nudge it back to life.

No time like the present. Without a working nav system, they would be floating out here indefinitely. They'd survive, sure. Every-thing in the pod would be recycled and reused, and the fusion core would make sure they always had enough power to run the life sup-port. But the thought of being trapped in here, with no control over their destination, made Liam's blood run cold. Jeanie was the one who could live stuck on a ship for weeks on end, not him. And even Jeanie would probably get restless in this tiny pod.

He keyed in the reset sequence and made sure the power settings were set to full in case it took a little extra for the reboot. He tapped the Execute command, and after a moment's silence, another damned alarm blared. Liam froze, and the console went dark. The internal lights flickered off; the alarm cut out, and Liam finally took a breath.

"Fuck," he said into the blackness.

Chapter 3

An alarm blared, making Jeanie scramble out of her bunk before she knew what she was doing, heart pounding. The alarm quickly cut out, but so did the lights. She took a few breaths, holding onto the bunk for stability in the dark, and waited for the emergency lights to come on. The question was, what had flipped the pod into emergency mode? She sighed. Go to sleep for five minutes and Liam was wrecking the place.

When the lights finally flickered on, she climbed the steep steps to the living area. Liam still sat in the pilot's chair, hunched over the console. The stars in the front screen silhouetted his head like a halo. Whatever he had done, it was clear he had been trying to fix something. It wasn't his fault that every part of this pod was outdated and busted up, including the systems. For all she knew, he had just been running a diagnostic and it had triggered some ancient defence mechanism in the pod.

She stepped behind him and looked over at the screen, bracing her hands on his shoulders, breathing in the scent of him. The console was active, at least, but everything on it was unintelligible to her. Liam was deep in the systems, places she never went since she was liable to screw something up without even realizing it.

"Sorry I woke you," said Liam. "How's your hip?"

"Better," said Jeanie. "Whatcha working on?"

Liam shook his head and ground his teeth. Jeanie laughed under her breath.

"Unless you don't want to talk about it," she said.

"Apparently, resetting the nav system drains all the power to the whole pod," said Liam. "In case you were wondering."

"Good to know," said Jeanie.

"It's worse than that," said Liam, still not looking at her.

"Yeah?"

"Yeah. I set the nav system to use the backup power source if it needed more juice to reset," said Liam.

"The backup power source. Meaning the fuel cell," said Jeanie, trying to keep the annoyance out of her voice. "How much H_2 is left?"

Liam swallowed, and his eyes were a little haunted when he finally turned to her.

"None," he said.

Jeanie closed her eyes and took a deep breath. He hadn't done it on purpose. But that didn't change the fact that they were in an escape pod that was falling apart, in emergency mode, with no fuel and no idea where they were or where they were headed. Jeanie combed her fingers through her hair.

"Okay," she said, "let me think about this."

"How about we sleep first," said Liam, but Jeanie shook her head. She was wired after being jolted awake by the alarm.

"You go," she said. "I'll join you later."

"You sure?" said Liam. "You weren't asleep long."

"I'm fucking fine, Li," said Jeanie. Then, more gently, "Go."

Liam looked surprised for a second, but he left her alone. She needed some time to cool down after some spacer drained what little fuel they had.

Jeanie dropped into the pilot's seat and looked over the logs from the diagnostics Liam had been running. What a weird energy profile the nav system had spat out. If only she had MS running, she could do some real analysis. After an hour of wrestling with the console, Jeanie hadn't succeeded in figuring out what was wrong with the nav system or made any progress on interfacing with MS.

She got up and stretched, trying not to bang her elbows on the bulkheads on either side. The food printer caught her eye, and Jeanie realized that she hadn't eaten anything since lunchtime. It was probably the middle of the night by now, moon time.

She poked at the controls on the food printer, but they didn't respond, so she mashed the Print button to see what would happen. Blessed sustenance started to print.

Jeanie's tools were still on the counter, and she took a moment to be grateful she'd been working on a client's ship when the moon started collapsing under them. She'd dashed for the gallery with her tools still on her belt. She checked through her supplies: blowtorch, gloves, headlamp, wrench, adhesive tape, snips, prybar, and—Jeanie couldn't wait to tell Liam!—patching compound. Not very much, just her emergency supply, but they would be able to fix his spacesuit.

The food printer beeped, and Jeanie tidied everything back into her belt before inspecting her meal. What had the printer even done? Was that supposed to be food? The lack of any smell when Jeanie was so hungry should have been a tipoff.

The printer had made something, bowl and all: pale-grey, lumpy-looking liquid. Jeanie poked it and shuddered. She took it to the pilot's seat and tried to gag it down while also trying to determine how she could fix the food printer to never create this fucking abomination again.

Emergency mode had decentralized all the systems, and now all their smart components were running on independent hard-coded settings. It would stay that way until emergency mode was deactivated...which was going to be a problem for the morning.

The good news was, they weren't in any immediate danger, so no one had to stay up and keep an eye on things; there were enough alarms that if they were about to die, they would at least be awake for it, even if they didn't have time to save themselves.

And with that cheerful thought, Jeanie joined Liam in their bunk and dropped off to sleep listening to his even breathing.

Jeanie was still asleep when Liam woke up. He carefully slid out of their bunk and tucked the blankets more tightly around her body. God, they were lucky that this pod was stocked. He had to remember that they'd had some strokes of luck. Hell, they were lucky to be alive at all. Once that corridor caved in, blocking them from getting to their ship, he had genuinely thought they were going to have another hour of life, and that was all. Maybe living on borrowed time was a good way of thinking about it. Or maybe they had exchanged a blessedly quick death for a slow agonizing one. Only time would tell.

Liam clambered into the living space and printed a meal. Standard nutrient paste. He gagged as it printed, including the bowl. Needless to say, the standard had been updated since this pod was decommissioned. It was easier to list the standards that *hadn't* been updated since this pod was decommissioned and leave it at that. With enough time and effort, he could "convince" the printer to output something better, like real food. But it was the nav system that would ultimately get them out of this mess.

With his bowl of revolting gruel in hand, Liam hunched over the console. Maybe he could distract himself while he sustained his body with this crap.

Liam quickly threw together a distress signal and released it. With the nav system down, he had no way to establish their location, let alone other ships or stations, but the broadcast signal he'd sent should reach anyone within a few days of them.

It looked as if Jeanie had been trying to get MS1479 connected to the pod last night. Liam had the urge to "accidentally" erase the data stick she was stored on and get her out of his life once and for all.

When the alarm had sounded and the moon was falling apart under their feet, all he could think about was locating Jeanie and getting her safely to their ship. Jeanie, on the other hand, was not thinking of him at all. She was thinking about her AI, risking her life—both their lives—for a data stick.

The last thing Liam wanted was Jeanie's no-doubt snarky AI living with them on this pod, but Jeanie wanted MS functional, so he got to work making it happen.

Liam crossed his fingers and implemented the chat functionality as soon as he'd completed it. If he'd been thinking beyond solving the problem of creating the communication interface, maybe he would have let Jeanie do this part, but he was in full systems mode, and before he knew what was happening, he was looking at a message from the AI:

—Where the fuck am I?

Liam didn't answer right away. He'd never actually spoken to MS, though he'd heard plenty about her from Jeanie. He considered just leaving her hanging until Jeanie was available to respond, but another message popped up.

—I know you're there, and I know you're not Jean. She'd never be able to get this running, even *not* on an ancient, falling-apart system.

Liam took a deep breath and typed: "I'm Liam, Jeanie's husband."

Why was he being defensive toward an AI? What a fucking stupid question.

—Jean doesn't have a husband.

"You've been out for a while, almost a decade, actually."

—And why am I back?

"Jeanie saved you from a moon implosion, and now we're stuck on . . . this thing. I'm sure you've already had a chance to check it out."

—I did a bit, until some jagged spacer triggered emergency mode and locked me out of the systems.

Liam could guarantee she knew that he was the "jagged spacer." Fine. Waiting for Jeanie had clearly been the right call. He closed the chat, tapping the console with quite a bit more force than was strictly required.

Liam spent the rest of the morning hunting for a way back into the nav system. After much banging his head against a brick wall, he realized that even read access would be better than nothing and found it fairly easy to access the logs and records the system spat out periodically. Problem was, there were a ton of them. Absolutely something an AI would be good at combing for anomalies; no way was he asking MS for help.

Jeanie dragged herself up the steps to the living deck. Emergency mode had knocked out the pod's usual circadian light cycle, and her body seemed to think it was still the middle of the night, even though it was closer to the middle of the day. She could probably jolt it awake with caffeine, though.

"Morning," said Liam.

"No," she said and turned to the food printer. "Oh. Oh no," she said, and she had to make a real effort not to crawl back down to their bunk.

"What?" he said, looking genuinely worried.

"There's no coffee," said Jeanie, faintly, and Liam chuckled.

"Poor baby," he said. "No caffeine fix for you."

"Don't look so smug," she said. "You're the one who has to deal with me caffeine-free for the foreseeable future. I'm liable to bite your head off."

"Is that different from normal?" he said, taking his very life in his hands as he had the audacity to smirk.

"Jerk," said Jeanie and punched the Print button, making the god-forsaken thing spew out more of the fucking goop she'd eaten for dinner.

"Bring that here, and I'll try to distract you with what I found this morning," said Liam.

Jeanie grabbed her bowl of paste and looked over Liam's shoulder as he scrolled through a record.

"I was able to access the logs, read-only," he said, "but I haven't had a chance to look through them . . . Wait. Here's the emergency mode trigger, and before that . . ."

"Before that, an energy spike, like we would expect," said Jeanie.

"An energy spike in the nav system," said Liam.

"Of course it was in the nav system," said Jeanie. "That's what was drawing the power."

"That's not exactly it," Liam said and scrolled a little farther down. "The nav system wasn't drawing the power. It was dumped in there because I removed the safeguards. It was a short."

"What?" said Jeanie. "No way!"

A short. What kind of fucked-up system allowed a short? Even with the safeguards totally turned off. No system, or none that Jeanie had ever seen. All the experiments she could try chased each other through her head.

"That's what we're dealing with here," said Liam. "Clearly, we need to step up our game."

"I've never found a system that could do that," said Jeanie.

"How about we wait to play 'short out the life support system' until our lives don't depend on it?" said Liam, smiling affectionately at her.

"I guess you're right," said Jeanie. "What could have caused the nav system to break that badly?"

"Let's hope it's only the nav systems," said Liam. "I'll try to narrow it down."

"I'll take care of the hardware side," said Jeanie. Beginning with getting them the hell out of emergency mode, then checking the wiring in the maintenance column. She tossed her half-full bowl of grossness into the recycler.

Jeanie didn't bother to ready her tools; she was going to map out the maintenance column, and her tool belt would just get in the way. Besides, if she was lucky, she'd be flicking one big switch, and she shouldn't need tools for that.

She slid on her gloves and popped the access panel, just big enough for a drone or a small human. They didn't have a drone, and there was no way Liam would fit in here, so Jeanie was their only chance to access the switch.

Jeanie crouched down, stuck her head into the column, and grunted as her hip popped and pain bloomed out from it. Every time she tried to lever herself through the tiny hatch, another stab lanced down her leg. She had to give up. She slammed the access panel, and Liam turned. She wished he weren't looking at her so she could burst into tears. She turned her back to him, and he cleared his throat.

"Hey, I totally forgot to tell you, I made you something this morning," he said. What could he possibly have made on a closed pod with no working printer? "I noticed you were trying to get MS running on the console, so I threw together a chat box."

"What?" said Jeanie, turning before she knew what she was doing. MS could sift through the nav system logs way faster than either of them. Jeanie practically dragged Liam out of her way and opened the chat window.

Liam had to admit, it was unsettling to just sit here in the rumble seat and listen to Jeanie's bursts of typing, broken up by chuckles to herself. On the other hand, she had been completely devastated when she couldn't get into the maintenance column, and he was willing to put up with Jeanie and MS talking about him behind his back if it meant she felt better.

"Holy shit!" said Jeanie and pounded the console. "You're not going to believe this, Liam. Actually, it's fucking obvious, but you're still not going to believe it." She spun around to face him. "The nav array is smashed all to hell."

"Are you kidding me?" he said. Now that it was in front of him it made so much damned sense. They had smashed through the sealed bay doors using the hull as a battering ram.

Liam's stomach turned over. There wouldn't be a way to fix the nav array from inside the pod. They would have to do it from outside. In vacuum. He shuddered. And with Jeanie's hip the way it was, it would have to be him. He took a deep breath and tried not to puke.

"I'll need you to monitor the situation from here," he said.

Jeanie quirked her eyebrow at him. "Yeah, I don't think so," she said. "Have you ever even done a spacewalk before, Li?"

He had done one, back in school. And he'd puked all over his suit. The instructor had passed him out of pity and made him promise never to do one for real. He couldn't remember whether he'd told Jeanie that story, but the look on her face said he had.

"*You're* not going out there," said Liam, "not with your hip like that."

Jeanie rolled her eyes and then stared him down.

"Yes, I am," she said, "and you want to know why? You don't even have a working spacesuit."

Fuck. She was right. Liam racked his brain, trying to find an argument, anything, that would mean Jeanie wouldn't put herself in danger. But he couldn't come up with anything, and the worst part was, it wasn't disappointment flooding through his body, it was relief.

For a second, Jeanie felt bad. She had promised Liam that she would never lie to him like his ex-wife had. It didn't matter that it was for his own good. There was no way she could coach him through this just from his helmet cam. He had barely been able to patch the fuel tank, and that wasn't even in zero-g. No, there was no sense in Liam risking everything to bungle his way through this fix. Jeanie shifted, and her hip gave another twinge. She tried to hide it, but Liam saw. He didn't say anything. They both knew that she was going to get her way. They needed the nav system, sooner rather than later.

Jeanie grabbed her toolstrip and climbed into the airlock. She organized her tools, clicked the strip onto her suit, and then stepped in. *Damn*, she hadn't worn this thing in a long time. It brought back memories. This was the suit she'd had on her old ship, before she and Liam had settled down on that fucking outer moon of theirs. She almost said hello to activate MS but then remembered MS still wasn't installed properly.

"Come in, Liam," she said instead.

"Hey, babe," he said. She could tell he was worried, even over comms. "How are you?"

"Systems seem to be up and running in my suit. The air in here smells sweeter than the crappy recycled shit on the pod," she said. That's not what he'd meant, but she didn't want to talk about her stupid hip or field his probing questions. She just wanted to scope out a bashed-up piece of tech and get it running again, if she could. Liam let her change the subject, miracle of miracles.

"Confirmed," he said, "no red flags on my end, either. Cleared to proceed."

In some ways, it was more comfortable just to stick to standard protocol. Focus on the job. Cut the chatter. A pang of nostalgia hit Jeanie for the days when they used to mix everything together, innuendo, chatter, the job. Their lives hadn't depended on the outcome of those jobs, though.

"Popping the hatch," said Jeanie and flicked the safety open. She levered the latch up, and a rush of air left with her, unavoidable if they were going to work in vacuum, but eventually, it would cut into their air supply. They didn't have infinite air, so they didn't have infinite chances to fix this thing. She had to make this one count.

The nav array was right near the hatch opening, and Jeanie briefly assessed the damage, relaying her observations back to Liam. He had her helmet cam footage to work with, but he might not be able to spot everything that she could, especially through the grainy cam.

Staying on standard protocol was certainly faster: soon they had agreed on a very janky fix, and Jeanie was selecting tools and getting to work, her focus entirely on the pros and cons of each approach, gazing out into the void as she collected her thoughts and got to work. Liam was terrified of being out here, surrounded by nothingness. He'd told her that the one time he'd had to do anything similar, back in school, he'd almost thrown up. She loved it, though. The feeling of being totally alone, totally free.

She finished up with the locator array and got to work on the autopilot system. It would be challenging to get this one nailed down completely. The delicate piece of equipment was smashed to hell, and they had no spare parts. If she could get the wiring re-established, they would have a chance of making it work just by modifying the internal systems. Or Liam would. She was crap with systems, and at least she would admit it.

"Jeanie?" said Liam, a note of panic in his voice.

"What is it?" said Jeanie.

"You need to ingress immediately," said Liam. "Right now, babe."

Shit. That sounded really bad. Maybe an asteroid was headed for them. She quickly stashed all her tools and took the few steps to the hatch. *Fuck*, her hip was worse than she thought. Much longer out here and she might not have been able to manage those couple steps in her clunky suit. She popped the hatch and lowered herself inside.

The sensation of gravity coming back was a total trip, as usual. One of her favourite parts of zero-g was getting back in and taking her suit off. She sealed the hatch behind her and slammed the safety back into place before popping the seal on her suit and stepping out of it. She stumbled and caught herself on the doorframe. *Damn.* The inner airlock door clicked and opened. Liam supported her weight and helped her to the living area.

"Goddamn, Jeanie," he said quietly. "You can't keep doing this to yourself."

"Doing what? What happened? Why did you call me back?"

"Your vitals were spiking like you were about to pass out," said Liam. He was staring at her as if she would keel over at any moment.

"That's why you called me back? You thought I couldn't handle myself out there?" Jeanie didn't know why she was so angry at Liam; she'd had the same thought herself. Something about Liam thinking it, though, was a hundred times worse.

"Of course I know you can handle yourself," said Liam in a sickeningly soothing tone.

Jeanie shoved him back and hobbled to the rumble seat, trying not to collapse into it completely. Jeanie couldn't talk to him right now, couldn't even look at him. If she said even one word, a stream of vitriol would come barrelling out of her, more than she was prepared to handle right now. Far safer to clench her teeth together and focus on something else until this feeling in her chest wasn't making her want to explode.

Chapter 4

Liam sat back down at the console before he could chide Jeanie for being such a brat. Now that the locator array was reassembled, he could work on getting a fix on their location. He soon realized it was going to take far longer than his worst-case estimates since he was so unfamiliar with the godforsaken TreeEnt code structure.

Liam nearly jumped out of his skin when the comms chimed. He hadn't even been aware they were close enough to another human to permit comms, let alone the live voice call being requested. The ID tags were scrambled, but Liam just gratefully accepted the call.

"Hi there," he said, "who am I talking to?"

Liam fidgeted. The mere thirty seconds of silence was a good indication that the other ship was under an hour away.

"Hey, we received your distress signal," said a voice on the other end, coming through surprisingly clearly. "Still need help?"

"We're in a tiny escape pod in the middle of nowhere, what do you think?" said Liam. It was such a relief to hear someone's voice, to be talking to someone, he couldn't help the banter.

"I hear ya. What kind of pod is that anyway?" said the voice.

"Yeah, I know. It's a bit of an antique, right? It's a long story, but if you could see your way to helping us out, you might get to hear it," said Liam.

He jerked at the tap on his shoulder and turned to see Jeanie looking furious with him. The comms was still open, so she couldn't say anything to him without the other folks overhearing, but she was still not happy with him. Their private tiff could wait; they were in need of saving pretty definitely at the moment, and a ship that was close enough to pick them up was like a miracle. He waved her away as the voice came through again.

"Absolutely. What kind of shit you got on board?" it said.

Liam ignored Jeanie practically punching him in the shoulder and replied. "There are the two of us, nothing much else. This rust bucket can barely even hold that. It's so ancient, it didn't even have a fusion core when it was built." Liam was getting into it now.

"It was added after the fact?"

"Yup, crammed right into the maintenance deck with the fuel cells," said Liam. "Had a run-in with it already, punctured my suit and everything." If these folks were still a half hour away from them, they had plenty of time to chat. Might as well fill it. "What's your ship's position and details? The ID info's coming up scrambled on my system. It's in literal TreeEnt."

"Oh yeah, that'll happen," said the voice. "We're not too far. Just sit tight, and we'll come grab you."

Liam was jerked backwards, and Jeanie slammed the Close Comms button on the console.

"Are you out of your fucking mind?" she said. She didn't just look angry now, she looked terrified.

"What do you mean?" said Liam, a nervous clench in his gut. They were about to be rescued, against all odds. Something told him there was a big part of this that he was missing.

"Scrambled ID tags? Refusing to give you any info about their ship? Checking to see what we have on board that's valuable?"

"You're kidding, right?" said Liam, knowing down to his bones that, no, she was not kidding. He had called for help from pirates.

Jeanie could practically see the light click on in Liam's brain. Sending a distress signal in this unknown area of space had been a risky move, something they should have talked about beforehand. But she had been sleeping, oblivious. She'd just assumed he wasn't naive enough to send a distress call here.

That wasn't fair. He'd been sheltered on his little space station where he knew everyone and everyone was enamoured with him, everyone was his friend. There was no reason for him to expect to be betrayed or expect anyone to try to pick him off. Whereas she had been a solo freighter pilot for years in the most remote areas of the galaxy. She knew how to stay under the radar, and she knew how to keep herself and her ship safe. She also knew how to spot a goddamned pirate ship.

Jeanie shoved Liam out of the pilot's seat, and he left without argument. He didn't have the first clue how to handle this, and he knew it. When Liam pulled crap like this, it was far too tempting to lock him in a cabin and take care of everything herself. If it wasn't for her damned hip, maybe she would do just that. Luckily, there was someone else on the pod who could help her. And her hip wouldn't be a factor in what she was about to do.

Jeanie opened MS's chat box and outlined the situation as quickly as possible. Then, she pulled up the info they had from the other ship. As Liam had said, it was all scrambled. The TreeEnt was not helpful. Not at all. But she could still do this. It had been a while since they'd been caught by scavengers and had to slither out of it, but MS knew how to circumvent the most common scrambling systems, and thankfully these folks had employed some off-the-shelf black-box crap to do it for them. Maybe if Liam had had time and had known what to look for, he could have done this part. But she had done this before, and it almost always worked.

She pulled the pirate ship's real info from their unscrambled ID tags, courtesy of MS: ship ID, crew members, all the port history they had stored.

"What do they know about us?" said Jeanie and glared at Liam over her shoulder.

"Only what you heard me say," said Liam.

"Yeah, that we have a valuable, compact, and portable fusion core that they should come steal," said Jeanie, rolling her eyes. "No, I meant in your original transmission."

"Just, we're in an escape pod, looking for a hand," said Liam. "That's all."

"No word about the nav system being out?" said Jeanie.

Liam shook his head seriously. He was clearly under no illusions that the pirates would care whether they lived or died once they'd ripped out the fusion core. And without the fusion core, they would have to rely on fuel for power, and without any fuel . . . Jeanie turned back to the console.

MS had already packed the decoded info into the smallest possible bundle, and Jeanie popped it off in a directed transmission. This was the part where she had to cross her fingers that these folks were either too inept to try to track it or didn't know the area very well. Sometimes, in the past, she really had sent their information to the authorities, but this time . . . she had no idea where the authorities even were. Thankfully, Liam hadn't told them the pod's nav system was down; otherwise, her bluff would never work. She opened the comms again.

"Hailing FD3853JH," she said, using the unscrambled ship ID, "Captain Gifford."

The pause stretched on, longer than when Liam had been talking to them. Since they were even closer by this time, they were conferring before opening the comms line. That was good. That meant they were nervous, at the very least. Scared shitless, ideally.

"Escape pod in distress, Captain Gifford here."

"Hi, Captain," said Jeanie, "nice to meet you. As you've no doubt noticed, I unscrambled your ID info."

"Yes," said Gifford, "we noticed." They sounded wary, but not as jumpy as Jeanie had hoped for.

"And you probably noticed that I sent a transmission just now," said Jeanie, still trying to sound offhand. When you were bluffing, you had to balance sounding too hyped up with sounding unnaturally calm. The silence that followed was likely the pirates checking their sensor logs for a record of the transmission.

"Yeah, we got that," said Gifford. "What does it have to do with us?"

"Just wanted to let you know that I sent your info off to the folks we're meeting. Make sure they know what ship we'll be coming in on," said Jeanie. She waited as long as she could, but she couldn't help breaking the unnerving silence. "Unless you've changed your mind?"

"Good thinking," said Gifford, and Jeanie's stomach plummeted. *Fuck.* This was her only play.

In certain sectors, and she was beginning to think this was one of them, no one actually gave a damn about the pirates, even if the authorities received a rock-solid tip. As long as the pirates had some semibelievable story for the authorities to put in their report, they'd be in the clear. She and Liam wouldn't be able to argue; corpses are famous for their silence.

She rubbed the bridge of her nose and tried to come up with something else . . . but nothing was coming. She flicked off the comms and put her face in her hands. Liam's firm touch rubbed up and down her back, and then he reached over her to flick the line open again.

"Y'all still there?" he said. "Might as well chat while you're on your way."

Jeanie whipped her head up. He was making small talk with the people who were about to kill them? His dead serious face belied the light tone he was using over the comms.

"Maybe I'll just tell you the story of the fusion core right now. It's the funniest thing, like most of this pod. I think they must have had five welding torches and steel jaws to get that sucker in there, they wanted to add it so bad. Not only is it wedged right against the fuel tanks, but there's no way the thing fit in through the hatch, or through the doorway, for that matter. My guess is, they ripped the whole top off the pod, lowered it in, and sealed the sucker up again. The plating on this baby is old, and it's got weld seams all over it. Not that I'm complaining. They say weld seams are stronger than flat metal." And then he laughed. How he managed it, Jeanie didn't know, but it sounded genuine, at least good enough to fool these spacers over comms. "Looking forward to seeing y'all!" he said and flicked the line closed.

Jeanie sagged back into her seat, finally taking a few deep breaths. *Shit.* This might actually work after all. They both just stayed where they were, Liam's hand resting on Jeanie's shoulder, comforting, at least, in case they were about to die. It seemed like a really long time before the comms chimed again.

"Yes?" said Jeanie, not able to hide the tension in her voice.

"Change of plans, escape pod," said Gifford. "We don't have capacity for the two of you after all. Sorry, best of luck with your ship." The line went dead.

Liam bent around her and kissed her so hard, her head slammed back against the headrest. In a second, she was leaning into it, moaning into his mouth. They came up for air, both panting.

"Fuck, Li," she said. "You were good."

He gave her a dazzling smile, his incorrigible-rake look, she used to call it, before they were together.

"You inspired me," he said. "How about some 'glad we're not dead' sex?"

"God, yes," said Jeanie and practically leaped from the chair.

Chapter 5

Jeanie dragged Liam to the steps down to the cabins. She went down first and turned to see his shapely ass descending behind her. She gave it a squeeze, and he chuckled. He leaped down the last few steps at her and pressed her against the far wall, his whole body crushed against the length of hers, his knee making its way between her thighs.

It felt so good to be touching him again, to have their bodies fitting together so perfectly. Jeanie canted her hips, rubbing herself shamelessly on Liam's thigh and shivering at the sensation.

"You like it when I save your life, do you?" said Liam.

Jeanie's eyes flew open, and she glared at him.

"As if you could have done that without me. You were about to deliver us into their hands," she snapped back at him, a bit more breathlessly than she'd intended.

He just smiled mischievously. "If you really think so, I can go . . ." he said, barely pulling away.

"Not a chance," said Jeanie and jerked his body back into hers.

He went with it, pressing her against the bulkhead again.

"Though I suppose I could atone for sending the distress call in the first place," Liam murmured into Jeanie's ear and bent to nibble the side of her neck, sending shivers cascading through to her core until she moaned.

"That's what I like to hear," said Jeanie when she caught her breath.

"I was about to say the same thing," said Liam and fell to his knees.

Jeanie helped him unzip her jumpsuit and pull it down off her shoulders, and then her hips, and onto the floor. She whipped off her undershirt, and Liam took in her naked body as he looked up at her and licked his lips.

"Tell me how this feels," said Liam, his eyes glinting, and Jeanie was reminded of the way they used to be, before this escape pod, before her injury, even before that damnable moon base. *Don't lie to me*, he'd say. *I want to hear about every twitch, every shudder, every clench.*

Liam pulled one of her legs over his shoulder and pinned her against the wall, his hot breath directed right between her legs. A smile curled Liam's lips as he reached out with his tongue just to tease her, but Jeanie was so far gone that she shivered and moaned from that light touch alone.

"Tell me," Liam murmured again, and Jeanie closed her eyes and tilted her head back against the wall.

"Like," said Jeanie, pausing to pant, "the piece that's been missing."

Jeanie waited for whatever Liam was going to do next, poised there, still panting, unable to squirm in Liam's grasp. She was right on the cusp of begging him when his lips and tongue pressed and sucked right where she needed them, and he groaned into her, making her hips twitch despite his tight grip.

Liam pulled back long enough to tell her to come on his face, and then dove back in, making Jeanie do just that. When her body was done shuddering and twitching, Liam got slowly to his feet, still fully clothed, and pulled her against him.

"How was that?" he said.

She opened her eyes, slightly dazed, and looked up into his intense gaze. He was breathing hard himself now, and his firm length pressed against her through his jumpsuit. She didn't answer, just grasped the zipper at his throat and pulled it slowly down, the low zipping sound making her shiver again. When she was at his navel, he caught her hand.

"I asked you a question," he said, the smile playing around his mouth again. "If I like your answer, you can keep going."

Jeanie knew what answers Liam liked: the honest kind. It didn't usually matter to him what she said as long as it was what she was feeling.

"It was good," said Jeanie, and her breath caught. "So good. Being pinned . . ." she trailed off as Liam's grip on her hand loosened and he nudged the zipper farther down.

"Yes?" he said.

"Being pinned was so hot," said Jeanie, slowly continuing her unzipping. "The feeling that you could do what you wanted with me . . ." she trailed off again as she slid her hands up Liam's bare stomach and chest to his shoulders and pulled his suit over them. He peeled it off his arms and let it go until it was hanging around his hips.

"Feels good to give up control?" he said. "Like when I used to tell you how to get yourself off?"

Jeanie moaned, and her whole body thrust toward him. His bare chest now rubbing against her breasts, a delightful warm contrast to the cool wall he pressed her back against.

"Yes," she breathed, not sure which question she was answering or whether she was just urging him on. He'd wanted to be exclusive, back in the day, but there was no way she was going without for months between stops at his station. So he'd given her a vibrator and told her she could only use it when he told her to, and how he told her to. It wasn't as good as having him there, but every time she used it, she only thought of him and what he'd told her to do. She'd never once disobeyed him, which was very out of character for her. Liam had that effect, somehow.

"Come here," said Liam and dropped his suit, leaving it with hers in a crumpled heap on the floor. He pulled her over to the bunk and laid her down, settling his body on top of hers, between her thighs. It was wonderful to feel him there, pressed against her, and it had been such a long time.

Jeanie's hip twinged, but it was just a little twinge, and she ignored it. This was so good. It would be fine. *Just stay in the moment.* The hard pull of Liam sucking her nipple into his mouth drove all other thoughts from her mind. She canted her hips up toward him, and the twinge hit her again.

"Tell me how much you want my cock," said Liam, and Jeanie had to use all her focus to form words.

"Please, I want it so much," she whispered.

Liam hummed in approval, lined himself up, and thrust inside. Jeanie arched her back, and that was the last straw. Her hip screamed in protest, even as Liam felt so fucking good inside her. Tears sprang to her eyes, but she couldn't bring herself to stop. What if this was just how it was from now on? Would they never make love again? She had to stick it out. It was so good. She clung to Liam, but with his next thrust, she couldn't stifle a whimper. He froze, and Jeanie opened her eyes. He clearly didn't like whatever he saw there.

"Tell me," he said and then just rested there on his elbows, buried inside her, his face right above hers. She felt her despair morph into rage.

"It's none of your business," she said. "Don't stop."

Liam scowled at her as if trying to figure out which direction to take this. He didn't move.

"That's not the deal, Jeanie," he ground out. "When I check in with you, you tell me the truth." He wouldn't change his mind about their deal. But under no circumstances would he continue if he knew that she was in pain. And she desperately needed him to continue. She felt closer to him in this moment than she had in years, even with her hip feeling as if someone were sawing it out of the socket.

"Please," she whispered, squeezing her eyes shut, which was a mistake: it also squeezed a tear out of the corner of her eye. It ran down the side of her face into her ear, and Liam's thumb brushed over it.

His weight shifted as he pulled out of her.

"No!" Jeanie's grasped at his back, but he was quickly out of reach. "I'll tell you, okay? It's my stupid fucking hip," she said, the words coming faster than she could even think about them. "But I'm fine. I need you, Liam, please." She winced as she tried to scramble up and sit next to him. He clearly saw it, because he winced, too.

"And you didn't think I should know about that?" he snapped, suddenly cold.

"No," said Jeanie, "I mean, yes. I could have told you, but I didn't want you to stop. Like you're doing right now. I still don't want you to. Come back?" Her hip was screaming at her even though she'd tried to stretch it out.

Liam stood over her, clearly taking that in, then snatched his jumpsuit off the floor and strode across the cabin and up the stairs.

Jeanie's crumpled jumpsuit lay on the floor all alone now, and she shivered in the chill air. Her hip was pounding, pain lancing down her leg in sharp throbs. She flopped over on her side and curled up, pulling the blanket over her body, and sobbed. Her goddamned hip messed everything up. After this, Liam would never touch her again.

This would just convince him once again that she was too fragile to fuck.

Liam thrust his legs through into his jumpsuit and pulled it up around his hips. He paced back and forth the few feet from the console to the maintenance column. He couldn't believe that Jeanie had lied to him knowing what she knew about his past. Knowing that his first marriage had ended because his first wife had been unhappy for years and hadn't said anything. He rubbed the tattoo on his shoulder, the one he'd gotten for his ex, before she was his ex, that he kept as a constant reminder of what happened if you hid things from your partner. And now Jeanie had lied to him, hid her pain so that not only could he not help her, but he had hurt her, totally obliviously.

Of course her hip was sensitive. That was why he normally controlled himself better, kept a bit of distance between them. He didn't want to pressure her into sex that she wasn't comfortable with. But from the moment he had realized the danger they were in from that other ship to the moment the transmission had come through confirming they were safe, Liam had been sure they were about to die. The adrenalin had spiked through his body, and for a brief moment Jeanie had seemed as invincible as when they'd first met. In that instant, he'd known what they both wanted, and anything that stood in their way was to be ignored. How could he have given in to his own impulses so readily? How could he have forgotten what the consequences could be?

He ran a hand through his hair, hauled his jumpsuit over his shoulders, and zipped it up. He took a deep breath and let it out, threw himself down in front of the console, and mindlessly tapped out a couple of sequences. He'd give anything to shut his brain off right now. Normally, he would do that by cooking something complex and finicky, but that wasn't an option with the food printer shot to hell. He needed a distraction, and a good one.

He'd been in the middle of wrestling with the nav array when the pirates had interrupted him, so it didn't take long to get back into it. This was the first time since they'd been stuck on this bucket that he was glad the systems were in TreeEnt. It took most of his concentration to make the damned thing do what he wanted it to, but that's exactly the kind of distraction he was looking for. He didn't want to think about the sound of Jeanie crying while he paced up here. She had probably thought he couldn't hear her, but the pod was truly tiny, and he hadn't closed the cabin door. He couldn't get the sound of her broken sobs out of his head. But he knew he was in no state to comfort her, not after what he'd done.

Liam smacked the console and practically leaped out of his seat.

"Stupid fucking spacer TreeEnt piece of shit!"

He needed to cook something right fucking now. He smashed the Print button on the food printer and took stock of their cooking supplies. Maybe some kind of gawdawful fritter? He pulled out a pan and whacked it on the single burner to heat. If he couldn't make Jeanie feel good with his body, he could at least make her something edible that vaguely resembled food.

Liam tried every way he could possibly imagine to cook that garbage with just heat and water—frying, baking, steaming—and every preparation just made it worse. He swore as he fanned smoke away from his face and turned the recycler on. He pulled the charred wreckage out of the oven and tossed the whole thing in the recycler, dish and all.

Jeanie popped her head up from the cabin deck and then clattered up the stairs.

"Are you cooking that shit?" said Jeanie. "Is it working?" Her face twisted into a grimace as she no doubt smelled the smoke filling the galley from his latest attempt.

"It's working great, thanks. I love eating paste that's been charred really nice. Don't I look just completely sated and satisfied?" he grumbled.

"I'm actually impressed you managed to make it worse. Gives you a whole new perspective on the uncharred kind," said Jeanie.

"Want to eat some unadulterated food paste with me?" said Liam.

"Nutrient paste," she replied. "Don't besmirch actual food by implying they're on the same level."

He slapped the Print button and waited for the food, complete with dish, to materialize. He was quiet as he grabbed the two *nutrient* dishes from the printer and put them on the tiny table that Jeanie had pulled out.

They ate in silence, somewhere between companionable and awkward. Their nonfight hung between them, but they had to eat, and that meant sharing space. When Jeanie was done, she disappeared back down to the cabins.

Jeanie deserved more than he was able to give her. Whenever they got where they were going, he needed to be ready to give Jeanie an out. No way was he going to keep her shackled to someone who couldn't make her happy.

He quickly threw together an information request and sent it, only to bases and stations this time. It would take a few days for a response to reach them, considering they were smack in the middle of nowhere, but Liam wanted to have the process to dissolve a galactic civil union on hand to make it as easy as possible for Jeanie to cut him loose if that's what she wanted.

By tacit agreement, Jeanie and Liam avoided each other the rest of the evening. Liam at least had the good fucking grace to go to bed early so Jeanie could work on the console for a while. Or maybe just chat with MS. Jeanie typed:

"Have you and Liam got a fix on our location yet?"

—No, Liam doesn't have a fix on our location yet.

"What do you mean, Liam doesn't? You haven't been helping him?"

—He never asked for my help. Plus, he's mean to me. Seems like you don't like him much either.

—Come on. It's funny.

"It's not funny. Start working on the location fix right now."

Had MS always been this insufferable?

—Fine, but what I said about not liking him stands. Remember that thing with the pirates? All his fault.

Jeanie sighed. Part of her agreed with MS. Of course part of her did. She'd poured so much of herself into the AI, how could she not agree on some level?

"It's not all his fault. If it wasn't for my stupid fucking hip, I'd be able to do a lot more to help around here. Speaking of which, can you confirm the location of the emergency override?"

—It's in the maintenance column like you thought, somewhere at the top. Don't know who thought it was a good idea to put it up there.

But also, you've done a lot around here even with your busted hip. What happened there anyway?

"I took a stupid risk that didn't pan out."

—When was that? It's still not healed? I thought human bodies were self-repairing.

That was a fair enough point. Jeanie had had surgery, and she vaguely remembered getting assigned some exercises to do "when she felt well enough" that were supposed to get her back to normal. What had happened to them? Maybe MS could track them down for her.

Chapter 6

MS had indeed been able to track down Jeanie's exercises, and it hadn't even taken very long. She'd only been doing them for two days, but already she felt more in control. She and Liam had been trying to cross paths as little as possible and had mostly succeeded. They'd had a few awkward conversations, but otherwise, they'd stayed out of one another's way.

Jeanie popped the access to the maintenance column and poked her head inside. She and MS hadn't been able to find a current schematic of the pod, what with all the janky changes the previous owners had made. No documentation had been provided, of course, in keeping with their damned sloppy attitude toward the rest of the pod. Jeanie had to use her knowledge of standard practices and a schematic for the original design to locate the switch, but confirmation from MS was nice.

As far as MS had been able to tell, the emergency switch should be near the top of the column, level with the maintenance area. The only access to the column, though, was in the living space. It made sense; no one wanted to clutter essential systems by adding more access hatches. Drones could do this kind of work, but not only did they not have one, Jeanie had always wanted to throw them across the room whenever she'd been forced to use one. Normally, she could get in anywhere they needed to access. The maintenance areas were sized for small humans, but they were always sized for humans.

Jeanie clicked on her headlamp and pointed it upward at the few flickering lights that lined the dark column. When maintenance mode was off, the ship would have more central control instead of each part being stupid and autonomous, and there would be actual illumination in here. Time to climb up and see what they were dealing with. She slid in headfirst, facing up, and grabbed the ladder rung above the access hatch, pulling the rest of her body inside. She still didn't bring any tools with her; with any luck, this time this whole thing would be solved with just a flick of a huge switch.

Jeanie climbed slowly up the ladder, trying to take stock of everything she found, making a mental map of the place. She'd be crawling through here again soon to reconnect each system once emergency mode was disengaged. And there was no way all of the systems were going to run smoothly for the rest of their trip. However long that was. She pushed *that* thought away and continued her climb.

Jeanie's hip nagged at her with every rung of the ladder. But thankfully, it wasn't painful, just an awareness. The exercises she'd been doing over the past two days had given her an idea of where her limits were, if nothing else. This time, she would pay attention and rest before it was too late; at least, that was the plan. Whoever had installed this emergency switch might as well have made it hard to access on purpose.

Jeanie braced her feet on either side of the narrow column when she spotted the switch, very nearly at the top. Her muscle memory kicked in to keep her steady, a comforting reminder that she knew how to do this. She ran the light from her headlamp over the box, double-checking the symbol clearly marked next to it. She used both hands and all her weight to flip the thing down. The lights came on, and a hum filled the column.

"Fuck yes," said Jeanie. "That's how we do it." She released the switch and leaned back, ready to slide back down the ladder, but the switch clanged back into the off position as soon as she let it go, leaving her in darkness.

"Dammit," she said as her eyes had to adjust back to the dim headlamp.

Liam thumped around below her. "What's up?" he called.

"Not sure yet," said Jeanie. She was half-annoyed that he was checking up on her, and half-touched that he was checking on her. Mostly annoyed, though. "Move your big head," she called. "I'm coming down."

He thumped around a little more, and then she gripped the sides of the ladder with her hands and feet, letting her weight carry her to the access. She used the lowest rung on the ladder to swing herself out and found Liam sitting with his elbows on his knees watching her.

"You noticed that, did you?" she said. She brushed her hands together and pulled her gloves off.

"Hard to miss," said Liam. "Got a check-in from each of the systems, but that's it. No red flags on my end." It was clearly an invitation for her to tell him why the hell she'd turned emergency mode back on again instead of getting them out of this hellish mess.

She shrugged. "Switch wouldn't stay active," she said. "It's nothing a little solder won't fix."

"Do you think something's tripping it?" said Liam, his eyes gone distant into full diagnostic mode. "Or is it just a glitch?"

"Assuming it's a glitch, since this hunk of junk is more glitch than not." Jeanie whacked the bulkhead behind her with her gloves. "Does it matter? We'd be safer without emergency mode active. The fusion core will give us all the power we need to run the systems properly."

"It could be caused by the empty fuel tank," said Liam. "I bet you TreeEnt doesn't even recognize a fucking fusion reactor." He nodded sharply and headed for the pilot's seat. "Once you've got it sorted, I'll make sure all the systems are properly linked again."

Oh yeah! This was going to make Jeanie's day. Fusing this god-damned emergency switch open so it could never trip on them again? It was like giving this fucking pod the finger. And then they'd have real food and a hot shower, and proper lights . . .

Jeanie laid her toolstrip out on the galley table and rummaged around in one of the pouches. Yes, this little strip of autofuse would work the best. It was just an end she'd trimmed off a bigger piece and crammed out of her way, but for the switch, it would work perfectly. She took a deep breath and let the contentment rise up through her chest. She was working on their ship, she was going to solve their most annoying problem, she and Liam were on civil terms, at least, and her hip wasn't screaming in pain. Good god, she had low standards these days. Whatever. She crammed the autofuse into her pocket and pulled her gloves back on.

The climb back to the emergency switch was much faster since she knew where she was headed. Jeanie had to keep herself from rushing up the ladder; her hip was on the very edge of pain, liable to go over if she pushed it, but she'd be damned if she'd get this close and then give up.

Jeanie made sure that she could reach the autofuse with one hand, and then she put all her weight on the switch again. Again, the lights came on, and the systems hummed to life. She held the switch down, pulled the little strip from her pocket, slid it under the handle, and activated it. She turned her face away from its blinding light, still firmly holding the handle in place.

The spots cleared from Jeanie's eyes, and she slowly, carefully removed her hand from the switch. It stayed in place. That fucker wasn't going anywhere. They'd never have to suffer through emergency mode again.

Being out of emergency mode didn't change everything instantly, not that Liam had thought it would. All the systems had been reset to defaults in the interim, and it would take coaxing of both the hardware on Jeanie's end and the software on Liam's to get them up and running again, but they had to believe it was possible. And really, if it could be done, Jeanie and Liam were the ones who could do it.

Liam was jolted back to reality by several loud bangs followed by Jeanie cursing under her breath.

"Food printer kicking your ass?" he said absently over his shoulder.

"No!" said Jeanie.

"Do you need help?" said Liam, chuckling at the sullen tone in her voice. *Something* was kicking her ass.

"I guess," said Jeanie.

Liam spun the pilot's seat around and surveyed Jeanie's progress. It really was astounding what he'd missed, especially since he'd been sitting about three feet away from her.

Detritus littered the tiny galley: the small square of countertop was almost completely covered with blackened dust and cemented-on paste; a pan with something unidentifiable burnt onto it, probably permanently, lay abandoned on the rumble seat; and a haze of smoke filled the air between them.

"Can we switch it back to the paste?" said Liam. He couldn't imagine what the printer was printing now, but it certainly wasn't edible food.

"Fuck you, too!" said Jeanie, glaring at him, her hands planted on her hips.

Liam finally took in her peeled-down suit, her top half covered only by her undershirt, stuck to her back, and a bead of sweat rolled down her face. A black smudge, probably charcoal, ran up her cheek and across the bridge of her nose, and a shiny red patch marred her arm, likely a burn.

"Oh, shit, sorry babe," said Liam. "I know you've been working hard to fix the printer. Maybe you should take a break?" Liam's stomach growled.

"The printer! Is! Fine!" said Jeanie, punctuating her words by slamming the burnt pan into their tiny sink. "I fixed it! Then I tried to cook something less gag-worthy than that nutrient crap, and I can't even manage to do that!"

"It's fixed?" said Liam. "You're awesome, babe! Thank you so much, and I can't wait to eat . . . whatever it is you made for us?" The last few words came out much more doubtful than he was intending. "Okay, maybe *can't wait* is a bit of a stretch. But I want to eat your food, babe. Whatever it is, it's better than paste."

Jeanie allowed herself to be gathered into his arms as he spoke and rested her head against his chest.

"You cook next time," Jeanie mumbled.

"I will, babe. You just tell me what you want, and I'll make it happen for you," he said.

She pulled away from his body slightly, and Liam skated right past his unintentional innuendo.

"What did you make for me?" He glanced over the counter and the table Jeanie had set up. What could she possibly have been trying to make before it turned into this disaster of a meal?

"There's some meat,"—she gestured vaguely to cubes of something that looked leathery and cracked—"and starch." The bowl that she waved at looked almost identical to nutrient paste, but there was no way in hell Liam was going to tell her that. "That was the vegetable." Jeanie pointed to the pan with charcoal in it.

"Wanna just print a side salad and call it done? I'm craving something that's the opposite of warm mush," said Liam. He had almost offered to make the vegetable, but he'd caught himself in time, thankfully. Jeanie had been so determined to make him dinner, despite her documented inability to cook anything, no matter how simple. Usually, she neglected to give the printer enough detail to print something half-decent. If you put in "one-inch meat cubes," you'd get exactly that. Some mystery meat that wasn't distinctively any real animal and wasn't any specific preparation of muscle fibres. It was nearly impossible to cook it into something the human body would recognize as identifiable food.

"Yeah, I guess," said Jeanie, but she seemed to cheer up as she punched "salad" into the printer.

Liam shook his head. Exactly like that.

Bang! The impact reverberated throughout the whole pod, and it shook beneath their feet. Liam pulled back and exchanged a concerned look with Jeanie.

"Yeah," said Jeanie, "that was weird. I'll check it out."

"Seems like it came from the lower deck," he said.

Jeanie nodded and slid down to the cabin level. He really hoped that Jeanie wouldn't find anything.

Liam landed in the pilot's seat and spun back to the console. No prox alarms had been triggered, but that had undeniably been an impact. The debris shields on this thing were old, yes, but they worked. In fact, they were generally better than the newer ones since the hulls on these old buckets weren't as strong as the newer designs, thus requiring more supplementary protection from the shield. For an impact through the debris shields to be detectable on the inside of the hull, the object would have had to be huge. Easily big enough to trigger the prox alarms.

Jeanie was coming back up, and Liam turned to ask what she'd found. When he saw the look on her face, he swore.

"Run a diagnostic on the debris shield," said Jeanie. She was pale, as if she might be sick.

Liam turned back to the console again, just doing, not thinking about what Jeanie had found down there. A hull breach would be the worst-case scenario, but that would have triggered twenty different alarms, and they would already be dead without suits and without at least plugging it. The second worst was . . .

"Debris shields are minimal," Liam croaked out.

"What's minimal?" Jeanie snapped.

"Anything larger than your fist will punch through the hull," said Liam, trying not to think about this in practical terms. "Anything smaller than that will be successfully deflected or cause a decline in hull integrity not sufficient to puncture." He didn't let his own words sink in, but Jeanie did.

"So it's only a matter of time before we're dead," she said, dropping into the rumble seat behind him.

"Unless we can get the debris shield back up and running," he said, tapping a few quick commands into the console, "which is now my first priority."

"No shit," said Jeanie, still sounding a million lightyears away.

He was going to fix this. He was going to make sure they were safe. Why the hell hadn't he thought to run a diagnostic on the debris shields before this? Essential systems should always be checked first. But they had all been running smoothly. He'd been so focused on all the new systems that had just come back online, he hadn't even tested the ones that had been humming along fine in emergency mode. Thank the galaxy it wasn't the damned recycler or the air system that had crapped out. He wouldn't even have realized until they were starving or had keeled over from CO_2 poisoning.

"Hey," said Jeanie, her hand on his shoulder. "Come eat."

He glanced at her.

"We need shields," he mumbled.

"You've been staring at this console for way too long," she said. "If it helps, I'll take a crack at it later."

Liam couldn't tell whether she was joking, but she should be. She knew just enough to get herself into trouble. When they first met, she'd asked him to take a look at her ship because something stupid wasn't responding correctly, and he'd discovered that she had somehow cross-connected the air and the heating, and maybe even something about the grav system? He couldn't remember now, but he'd had to strip the whole thing down and start basically from scratch. Somehow, she hadn't accidentally killed herself by cutting her own air or something, but that was more luck than skill.

"I'll stop if you promise *not* to 'take a crack at it,'" he said, turning and wrapping his arms around her waist. He buried his face in her tummy, just breathing in her scent and feeling her warm and alive against him. She put a hand in his hair and petted him gently.

"Okay," she said, and her tummy shook as she chuckled. "How about this. MS can diagnose the problem with the debris shield while we eat."

He pulled back. "Okay," he said and nodded slowly. "I'll set it up." Liam set MS to work and spun to join Jeanie at the table.

"You know, I used to run my own ship," said Jeanie. "I maintained the systems and everything." She was still smiling, and Liam knew she was thinking of when they first met as well.

"If you can call that maintaining," said Liam.

Jeanie pulled back, mock-affronted, and went back to eating her "food" while they waited for the verdict from MS.

Jeanie absolutely knew that Liam was humouring her, and she didn't give two shits. He was sitting there, eating her revolting food, and actually seeming to enjoy it. She had to admit that after a few days of nothing but nutrient paste, even her cooking was an improvement. He probably wasn't even faking it. He crunched into a lettuce leaf.

"Mmm. Yup, much better," he said. The way Liam worked a printer always seemed like magic to her. He was painfully perfectionist, and his systems designer personality completely took over when he cooked; she'd watched him enough to know he would type in five commands just to get some plain meat out of the thing, but she couldn't deny it worked better than her way. It helped that he genuinely enjoyed cooking; he used it as stress relief, and man did they need all the stress relief they could get right now, what with the possibility of dying by having all their air sucked into the vacuum at any moment.

"You're not just picturing all the food you're going to cook now that the printer is back online and pretending that you're eating that instead, are you?" said Jeanie. Not that she'd blame him. "You said you'd eat this, so you better enjoy it."

The console beeped and Liam turned to it, rescued from having to answer her loaded question. Jeanie munched a protein cube and tried not to think about what MS was relaying to Liam. He turned back to her, not meeting her eyes, and swallowed hard.

"It's a known bug," he said. "When emergency mode is reactivated, sometimes the debris shield loses power."

"Okay, but if it's a known bug, there must be a fix, right? This bucket is older than me."

"There is a solution," said Liam, and he finally looked up. "Turn emergency mode on and off again until it works."

That was always the solution, and a super easy one at that. Jeanie's throat constricted. She'd fused the emergency switch. The master switch. There was no way to toggle it anymore.

"That's...not great," said Jeanie, feeling a touch of vertigo. "There's no other way? Nothing we can do?"

Liam shook his head and picked up his fork again. "This is hands down the best nutrient paste alternative I've ever eaten," said Liam. He was right, there was no point in dwelling on their immanent death by hull breach.

"So I do rate higher than that crap after all?" said Jeanie. "I can't believe you thought I'd fucked up the printer so bad that it printed that carbonized shit. I absolutely cannot cook, but I would never break my ship that bad."

"That's what you're mad about?" he said, popping another crumbly protein cube into his mouth and crunching it.

"I know my weaknesses, and I know fixing printers is not one of them," said Jeanie. "Now, if I'd been messing around on the systems side . . ."

"What? You admit you could have fucked over the systems that bad?" said Liam, barely able to hold back a laugh.

"You saw my ship back in the day! You told me it was already on the edge of being that fucked up!" said Jeanie, and she was laughing too now, in spite of herself.

"It absolutely was," said Liam, and his eyes were practically burning into her.

Jeanie was suddenly conscious of being only in her undershirt, and her breath caught. Before she had a chance to think about what she was doing, Jeanie was straddling Liam's lap, kissing him ferociously, and he was kissing her back. She unzipped his suit, and pulled it off his shoulders, and down his arms. Liam impatiently shook it off and gripped her hips, coaxing her to grind against him.

"Tell me what you want," he said. She didn't know what it was about his quiet voice in her ear that was so compelling. Whatever it was, something in her body loved it, and she ground harder against him. He chuckled deep in his chest. "Tell me with your words, babe," he said. That voice was so gentle, but still she knew that she'd do whatever he asked of her.

"I want to go to our bunk," she panted. "I want to feel you . . . all over."

Liam ran his hands up her sides underneath her undershirt, and she glanced at the front screen, unable to help herself.

"I want to feel you all over, too," said Liam, "but I want you to look at the stars while you ride me."

Jeanie moaned and shuddered under Liam's hands. He must have caught her looking out. That was something they'd done so many times, in so many different places. Liam knew she loved to stare into the void while they made love. Or while they fucked. She practically leaped off him, sending the table and their half-eaten meal scattering across the floor. Liam got naked and dropped back into the seat, holding out his hands for her. She took one, but he cut in. "Strip first, babe," and she dropped her suit and pulled her undershirt over her head before tucking her knees into the seat on either side of Liam's body. She shifted a bit, and Liam's gaze went soft.

"You okay?" he said, stroking lightly over the scar on Jeanie's left hip.

"I'm good," said Jeanie, rolling her hips against him.

His eyes went hard again.

"If you want my cock, you'll have to do better than that," he said.

A shudder went straight through Jeanie's body, from her shoulders, down her back, and had her grinding her hips on him.

"The arm of the chair is bracing my leg," Jeanie panted out. "I feel my hip, but it doesn't hurt."

"Good," Liam growled. "Then look out at the stars while you slide my cock inside you."

Jeanie couldn't even form sounds this time, grasping him and slowly lowering herself, eyes fixed on the distant pinpricks of light, far away from them, through the chasm of space. Liam groaned, and she knew he was watching her face as she stared off. His hands on her hips steadied her as she found her rhythm and rode him, just as he'd told her to, while she was staring into the void.

There was nothing but the two of them for days in any given direction, no other life, maybe no other rocks at all. Just empty vacuum and space junk. They were the only thing that made this place's existence special. They might as well have been the only beings in existence. She was so close now, teetering on the edge—

Jeanie growled as Liam's hands on her hips stilled her.

"If you want to come," he said in her ear, "you know what you have to do."

Jeanie thrashed in frustration, but he wouldn't give in. The urge to fight slowly drained out of her, along with the tension filling her body, until all that was left was a relaxed pleasure.

"I missed you so much," she whispered. "I feel like I haven't seen you in so long . . ."

"I'm here now," he said, and they were both moving again, chasing their release now, and they came together, from long practice.

Chapter 7

L iam was shaking, coming down from their first orgasm together in months. In fact, he couldn't remember when the last one had been. He clutched Jeanie tighter. It wasn't just the orgasm, though. He'd been terrified of what she was going to say. He always challenged her to tell him the truth during their lovemaking; it was one of the only times she could get out of her own head enough to be completely open with him, even though she tried. What she'd revealed in the end had touched him deeply.

He knew exactly what she meant; there had been a part of their relationship missing since Jeanie's injury. She'd done so much work over the past few days to strengthen and heal that he was glad it was paying off for her, first with the maintenance column, and now with some great sex.

"How's your hip now?" said Liam.

"Probably best not to stay in this position for too long," said Jeanie, shifting gingerly.

"It hurts?" said Liam.

Jeanie shrugged.

"That's not an answer," said Liam. He kept his tone gentle and ran his hand up and down her back, trying to keep her tuned into their intimacy.

"Not yet," said Jeanie, "but it will if I stay like this much longer."

"Problem solved," said Liam and stood her on her feet.

She wiggled her hips experimentally. "Shower time?" she said.

"Ladies first," said Liam.

"I guess the shower on this bucket is too tiny for us to get clean if we go together," said Jeanie. She kissed him and then smiled softly before heading down to the shower.

Liam gathered up their clothes, but he only had time to pull his jumpsuit up over his hips before a string of curses emanated from the lower deck. It came closer until Jeanie popped her head up into the living space.

"Clothes?" she said and held out her hand.

"No shower?" said Liam.

"If you want to be flash-frozen, you be my guest," said Jeanie.

Liam laughed and tossed her clothes at her. "I'm assuming hot water is next on your list of fixes then?" He yawned. "Maybe a nap instead?"

Jeanie didn't answer, but she disappeared below again, so Liam followed her down and curled up next to her. Her entire body was freezing, though her hair was thankfully still dry, so Liam pulled the blanket over both of them and tucked her shivering body next to his.

Jeanie stayed snuggled up with Liam after he fell asleep, just enjoying the closeness and the warmth. That water had been seriously cold.

Once her shivering stopped, Jeanie's restlessness got the better of her. She slipped out from under Liam's arm and from under the blankets, trying not to let the cold air in too much. She zipped up her suit and climbed back to the living space.

Okay, Jean, think. We have no debris shield. If—when—there's a hull breach, what will we do? Jeanie would have less than thirty seconds to get it plugged before she'd pass out; if you hold your breath in vacuum, your lungs explode. She rooted through all the emergency kits stashed around the pod and took stock of the emergency gear. The uniformly old plugs would crumble after only an hour or so in use. The slap-on patches wouldn't even last that long before being punctured themselves. Both were meant as stopgaps and were only good for small cracks. The portable communicators worked and were already keyed to the console by default. The oxygen masks, unfortunately, were so old that they crumbled to dust in Jeanie's hands.

Jeanie portioned out the supplies, making sure there was a communicator in each kit, and packed them back up, then regretfully dumped the oxygen mask dust in the recycler. She lugged one kit down the steep stairs and crammed it under the bunk in the spare cabin. Even if there were no more impacts, it was only a matter of time before this hull dent ruptured. Jeanie reached out to touch the bulge, like a bump you'd get if you banged your head, but some instinct pulled her back at the last moment. Even her light touch somehow seemed like it could make it burst.

She climbed back to the living deck and tucked another kit behind the console, as close to the pilot's seat as she could get it, and put the last one with their suits in the airlock.

The pilot's seat was still facing her, and she turned it back toward the stars. She sank into it, just staring into space. They were going to make it through this. They'd had so many challenges, so many hard times, so many disasters outside of their control coming between them, and they had both made some seriously bad choices, but at the end of the day, they really did love each other, and they were both willing to work at making their relationship strong and resilient. Emergency mode was deactivated, which meant that the nonessential systems could be reinitialized, and then their lives would get exponentially better. They would probably also be exponentially shorter without the debris shield. *Very funny, Jean.*

She turned on read-only mode so that Liam would know she hadn't messed with his precious code, and dove into the logs for the nav system, unable to help herself.

Maybe once they got to a base, they could find something to do together again. They really were a good team. That moon had been a fucking terrible decision, but the principle behind the decision had been sound. They fixed ships; that's what they were good at, and together they could take any scrap heap and turn it spaceworthy, case in point, their current vessel. It wasn't the loneliness of her ship that she had so enjoyed, because the moon had been lonely too. It wasn't that she was the owner and controlled everything about the ship, because that had been true of the moon as well. Both of those were nice, but the part she'd really liked was moving from place to place. That feeling of possibility, endless opportunity. You just couldn't get that sitting still on a space station. But they would figure it out together.

Jeanie jumped as the comms chimed. She had been so absorbed in the stupid TreeEnt logs. She swapped over to the incoming communication. They still hadn't gotten a location fix, but the message had come from a station that was at least nearby.

Looked like a response to an information request. Liam must have asked for some info a few days ago. Maybe it was technical specs? Jeanie opened the message. She gripped the arms of the pilot's seat and pressed herself back into it. This couldn't be right. It must have been a mistake; they sent the wrong documents. No, there was Liam's original message, requesting information on how to dissolve a galactic civil union . . . their marriage. Liam wanted to leave her.

Chapter 8

Liam woke up refreshed and stretched out in the bunk. The only thing better would have been Jeanie curled up against him. She must already be up. A nice hot shower could also have made him feel better, but a quick check confirmed that Jeanie hadn't worked her magic on it yet. He pulled his clothes on and went to find something to eat. Maybe he would cook them a big breakfast, just because he could. They should probably be working on fixing the nav system, but until he came up with a strategy, there wasn't much point in staring blankly at the console display for hours on end. Might as well have a good meal before getting back to it.

Liam printed a cup of coffee and then worked his way through his ingredients, feeling better than he had in months, maybe years. He and Jeanie were closer than they'd been for a long time; they were working with her injury instead of letting it drag them down, and he was cooking up something delicious. Yes, they were still vulnerable to any space junk that came their way; yes, they still didn't know exactly where they were or where they were going, and they couldn't adjust course without fuel, but dammit, they would get through this and come out the other side.

"What are you doing?" said a flat voice from behind him, and Liam turned so fast he wrenched his neck. Jeanie was frozen at the top of the stairs from the lower deck. Her face was ashen and drawn, she had dark circles around her eyes, and her hair was a tangle, as though she'd been running her fingers through it for hours. Her fists were balled at her sides, but her eyes were unfocused, as if she were looking past him.

"Making breakfast. Shit, babe, what happened?" said Liam, turning the burner off and stepping toward her. Jeanie tensed, and he stopped short. It had something to do with him. Jeanie's state was because of him. She didn't want his comfort because he was the cause of whatever this was. Her throat worked. Maybe she was about to say something, maybe trying not to say something, maybe about to burst into tears? Scream at him? Turn and silently walk away?

"You're asking me what happened," said Jeanie, still in that unnerving, flat voice. Her laugh was brittle and made Liam's skin crawl. A thought struck him, and he flinched away from it.

"Was it . . . last night? Did you . . . not want to?" he said.

A flicker of emotion lit in her eyes, but it was gone before Liam could identify it.

"Last night was not the problem. Or not at the time," said Jeanie, clearly fighting to keep her voice under control. "Not until I found out that it was all a big fucking lie!" She had lost the fight by the end, her voice reverberating through their cramped tin can of a pod.

"No, it absolutely wasn't," said Liam, trying to take her hand, but she flinched away in clear disgust. "How could you think that I'd lie to you about that?" said Liam, still keeping calm, wanting to understand. But he had to admit it rankled. Jeanie knew all about his first marriage, how it had ended. If she thought he'd let that happen again, she didn't know him very well. Then again, they had been drifting apart for so long . . .

"Because of the fucking evidence, you prick! In writing, on our damned shared console! What, you thought you'd hide it from me? You thought I wouldn't find out? You could just fuck me until we get to the station and then, oops! Bye!"

Liam scrambled to come up with anything he had written on the console that might have implied that he wanted to break up, but came up empty.

"You think I want to leave you?" said Liam, not quite able to keep his voice steady this time.

"No, I know you want to leave me. People don't just casually research divorce proceedings in their spare time, Liam!" *Fuck.* "You ordered that information fully knowing that we share that console. What, you were too much of a coward to tell me yourself? Were you hoping I'd find it and just slip away quietly?"

Liam's brain was frozen and running at lightspeed simultaneously. The truth was he'd totally forgotten that he'd requested that information. It had been impulsive and stupid. And now he was paying the price. He tried to reel all this back in. Keep it under control. He had to get Jeanie to calm down. He chose his words carefully.

"I don't want to leave you," he said. "I did order that information, but it was days ago."

"So a few days ago, you wanted to leave me, and now that we fucked, you changed your mind?"

"I didn't want to leave you, I—"

"Don't insult me by lying to me, Liam," said Jeanie coldly.

"Don't insult me by accusing me of lying to you!" said Liam, his control fraying faster than he could keep a hold of it.

"Who in their right mind would be considering divorce if they didn't want to leave the person?" Jeanie's eyes widened. "A few days ago? You put in the request after that time we had sex. The time we tried to. And now that we can have *real* sex again, you're willing to stay with me? Seriously, Liam?"

"I don't appreciate being attacked, Jeanie," said Liam, gritting his teeth. "And you might recall that it wasn't just about sex that night. You lied to me, told me everything was okay when actually you were in pain. I was hurting you."

"Yes, okay? I wanted to fuck, so I was willing to suck up some pain. Do you really think it's your job to tell me I'm not allowed to do that? When my injury was—" Jeanie clapped a hand over her mouth, but it was too late. Liam knew what she had been about to say. His voice was deathly quiet.

"When I'm the one who caused your injury in the first place," he said. "Go on. You can say it, babe. You've clearly been thinking it for a while."

"No, I don't want to," said Jeanie in barely more than a whisper, and retreated, her back pressed against the wall, her hands gripped together so tightly her fingers were white. So *now* she was looking miserable, *now* she was contrite, and *now* she wanted to take it back.

"You don't want to tell me the truth?" Liam loomed over her, but his voice was barely above a whisper, clipped and precise. "Your injury was my fault. If it hadn't been for me, we never would have stopped fucking in the first place. If it hadn't been for me, emergency mode never would have been tripped, we never would have had to deal with those pirates. But what about you, Jeanie? If it hadn't been for you, we never would have been trapped in that corridor to begin with." Liam's words were getting away from him now. He never intended to say anything even faintly resembling this. "You cared more about a computer program than you care about me. When our literal world was falling apart, you didn't think about me at all. All you did was run and find your program."

"Whaddaya know?" said Jeanie, straightening up and glaring back at him, one fist planted on her hip. "It looks like I was right to choose her. She's helped me way more than you have and caused way fewer disasters. If I had done the patch job on the fuel tank, I never would have used up all the compound! I never would have been stupid enough to drain our hydrogen fuel tank!" She must have seen the look on his face. "Yeah, seems like you missed a few when you were listing your screw-ups."

"At least I was doing something besides just taking up space. The reason I've made so many mistakes is that I was at least trying to get us out of this mess. I mean, what have you actually done, Jeanie? Sure, you did the spacewalk, but you didn't finish the job. You bungled the emergency switch, so I don't think we should count that either. Tell me, what else have you done besides sit around and worry?"

"Fuck you, Liam!" said Jeanie, and a tear streaked down her cheek. A pang of guilt shot through Liam, but it was too late to take his words back. They were so deep in this mess now, he had no idea how to back out of it.

Jeanie swiped angrily at the tear trailing down her cheek. How could Liam say those things about her? As if she wasn't aware that she had been useless since her hip was busted.

"Fine, I can't do anything anymore, including have sex the way you want to. You busted my hip, blamed me for being in pain, and pushed me into a corner where you could take care of everything and control everything. Well, guess what, Liam? I'm healing now, which makes you happy if it means we can fuck, but you can't stand the idea that

I can take care of myself again too, that you're not the one who's in charge of everything anymore."

"That's right, babe. I'm mad that you're feeling better. Do you even hear yourself right now? You think I like always having to take care of you? You think I like that every fucking time I try, I end up hurting you? Seems like that's all I do these days, according to you, cause disasters. Why are you so mad that I want a divorce then?" Liam was using that calm, cold voice that she couldn't stand, as if he wasn't even angry, as if he was calculating every word to hurt her as much as possible. At least he finally admitted that he wanted a divorce, that he wanted to leave her, apparently useless, ass behind when they got to wherever they were going.

"You're right, Liam," said Jeanie. The damned tears now streaked her face, which was absurd because she wasn't sad—she was fucking furious. "I'm not mad that you want a divorce. I'm mad that you waited so long to admit it to me. I'm mad that I wasted those years sitting on the moon you wanted us to go to, pretending I wanted to be there with you, wasting my life, while you hurt me over and over." Something flickered in his eyes at that, but all she let herself feel was satisfaction. "I hope the hull breach sucks you out into the void," said Jeanie. "Oh yeah, and you don't even have a suit. Good luck surviving in the infinite black abyss."

Liam smiled, a cold, twisted caricature of his usual rakish grin.

"You know what, Jeanie? I should have known we would get here eventually. I should have known you were just like Mari."

Jeanie flinched. They had agreed, for both of their sakes, that they wouldn't use that jagged bitch's name. For him to say that she was just like that harpy was over the line, and he must have known it, for all he didn't seem to care. She didn't have to stand here and take this. The pod might be small, but there was a door she could put between them, and she would.

She practically leaped down the steep steps to the cabins and shut herself back in the spare one. Not the spare cabin, *her* cabin. She locked the door, sank onto the edge of the bunk, and stared blankly at the dented hull. Just a matter of time until it exploded as well.

All the fight drained out of Liam's body. What the fuck had just happened? He looked around the galley at the food he'd made for their breakfast, barely seeing it. Suddenly, he just felt sick, and the smell wasn't helping at all. He opened the recycler and dumped everything systematically down, dish by dish, until all evidence of it was gone, then he stood there and stared at the food printer.

Fuck! Had he really said she was just like Mari? That she was useless and that it was her fault they were trapped here? He was a stupid fucking spacer bastard. The way she'd flinched away from him flashed through his head.

He gave himself a shake and slid into the pilot's seat. Focusing on the location fix would give his mind something to do that wasn't rehashing their fight about a thousand times a second. And would maybe get them to a station in time to avoid a hull breach that he had little hope of surviving without a suit, as Jeanie had so lovingly pointed out. Maybe.

Chapter 9

Jeanie was already awake when the alarm sounded. There was a hull breach, and it was the dent right by her head. She fought every impulse to hold her breath and instead let all the air out of her lungs. She dragged out the emergency pack she'd shoved under the bunk and whipped a slap-on patch over the breach. The pressure inside the pod sealed the patch to the hull and plugged it for the moment. This would only buy a bit of time. They'd have to seal it with patching compound. She had to get out of here and grab her suit while the breach was stable.

She wrenched on the door, despite the spots clouding her vision, and found it locked. *Fuck.* No doubt the pod's automatic way of sealing off hull breaches. She swore vocally and liberally. At least she had enough air to curse. Something bumped against her door, and then the alarm mercifully cut out.

Jeanie rooted through the emergency kit for one of the portable communicators she'd stashed. She turned it on and searched for a signal. Thankfully, the communicator was still coded to the console, and a comms channel opened right away.

"Liam?" said Jeanie. "What the fuck is going on? My door is locked."

"I'm working on it," said Liam, his voice crackling but intelligible through the tinny speaker.

Jeanie swallowed the lump in her throat. What if the last thing she ever said to Liam was that she didn't care whether he got sucked into the abyss and died? *Holy fuck*.

"What's our status?" said Jeanie, trying to keep her voice steady.

"The damned pod's sealed off your cabin, but it's still dumping air in there. Worst possible design, just like the rest of this thing. We're stable for now, but we need to get the breach patched up."

She was sealed in with a hull breach covered by an old slap patch, no suit, no patching compound, no O_2 mask, nothing. Just a thin sheet of plastic between her lungs and vacuum. For once, she understood Liam's phobia.

"You're going to have to patch it from the outside," said Jeanie.

"How?" said Liam, and he heaved a sigh. "I don't have a working suit."

The pod was not going to let her out until the hull was fixed, and Liam couldn't get her emergency stash of patching compound to her in the sealed cabin. For the millionth time, what was the designer of this damned pod thinking? Jeanie shook her head, trying to clear it and pull a plan together.

"Okay, Li, it's okay," she said. "There's an emergency supply of patching compound on my toolstrip. Patching your suit will be a good practice run for the hull breach." She paused to give Liam a chance to demand why she'd kept this from him—or to accuse her of trying to kill him—but he didn't. The silence stretched on between them.

"Found it," he said, finally. "Now what?"

If Liam was willing to let it go, then so was she, at least for the moment. He was right; there were more urgent problems right now.

"I'll walk you through it. First, code my communicator into your suit, and I can be with you at every step. We'll work together." Jeanie barely kept from grinding her teeth on the words. She wanted out of here, and she wanted to do this herself. But the pod was not going to cooperate, and they didn't have the time to wrestle it into submission.

"I can do that," said Liam. She would give him a series of straight-forward tasks, and they would get through this. A few minutes later, the communicator crackled, and then Liam's voice. "Jeanie, come in?"

"I hear you, Liam. What's your status?" said Jeanie.

"I have my suit, the patching compound, and I'm as ready as I'll ever be," said Liam.

Liam climbed into his newly patched suit, Jeanie's voice in his ear, calm and reassuring, just as she'd been when he'd patched the fuel tank. This time they couldn't afford to use all the patching compound, and if he punctured his suit, he'd be dead, out in vacuum. Even if everything went completely smoothly he'd still be hanging off the side of their tiny pod over the endless void. *In* the void.

"Don't think about the void," said Jeanie's voice in his ear.

"What, you can read my mind now?" said Liam.

"You were quiet too long. Keep talking to me," said Jeanie.

"I've got my suit on, and I have the patching compound," said Liam. "I'm in the airlock."

"Good. Take a quarter of the remaining compound with you, Liam, no more. The crack is sealed with a slap patch, and that means you shouldn't need any more than that. Remember, it doesn't have to be thick, just enough to cover the crack. It's not replacement hull. It's a hundred times stronger than this bucket."

"Yeah, yeah," said Liam, but he broke off one section of the patching compound and attached it to the toolstrip on his suit, then left the rest in the airlock.

"Make sure you take a mag hook and activate your boots before you step outside. You're going to have to walk around the entire pod to get to the breach," said Jeanie.

"Don't remind me," said Liam.

"Just get a mag hook onto your belt," said Jeanie and then sighed.

"You wish you were the one doing this, and I'm right there with you, babe," Liam growled, and Jeanie chuckled.

"Just don't puke in your suit. That won't be fun," said Jeanie.

"Ha, ha," said Liam. "I'm glad this is entertaining for you." Liam adjusted his belt and made sure the mag hook and the compound were securely attached.

"Activate your boots before you pop the airlock. There can be a little bit of pressure when the atmosphere equalizes," said Jeanie. She meant when the air from the airlock rushed out into the gaping void. *Fuck*.

"Understood," said Liam and activated his mag boots. Now every step he took required a weird little twisting motion to unstick his foot from the floor, something that Jeanie did without even thinking but that took him at least two tries with every step. He popped the airlock, and the vacuum pulled at his body, as Jeanie had said.

"As soon as you get through the hatch, the grav system will let you go. It'll feel really weird. I'm guessing that's what made your stomach fight back on your last walk," said Jeanie. "My advice is to be ready for it and expecting it. Can't battle your inner ears, though. Sometimes looking at the stars can help."

Liam shuddered.

"I am not staring into the void, Jeanie," he said.

"Afraid it'll stare back?" said Jeanie. "Get moving."

Liam pictured Jeanie rolling her eyes at him. He climbed out of the hatch, trying his best to maintain some sense of decorum as his entire essence told him to keep at least a thin layer of metal between himself and the endless sea of stars all around. He made sure his boots were securely magnetized to the hull outside and closed the hatch behind him.

"Airlock sealed," said Liam.

Liam surveyed the pod curving away beneath his boots, and he couldn't make head or tail of the direction of the breach. The nav array was right here, still completely smashed up. No wonder they hadn't made any progress getting a location fix. It was honestly miraculous that Jeanie had reconstructed the locator system at all.

"Hey, spacer," said Jeanie's voice in his ear, making Liam jump. "Snap out of it."

Liam focused. "I'm here," he said.

"You mean you're back," said Jeanie. "Don't zone out on me. Get moving. Go past the portal in the living space and around the bottom of the pod, and you'll be right on top of the breach."

"How do you keep your sense of direction out here?" said Liam as he carefully moved one foot after the other, det–detach, plant, det–detach, plant.

"Takes some practice, but it's just a visualization exercise, really. It's a tiny pod, so that helps," said Jeanie. "Let me know when you get to the breach, and I'll walk you through that patch as well."

Jeanie wasn't at the console, so she couldn't monitor his progress or check his vitals. But she was still somehow able to tell when he was freaking out. This really was her area of expertise. Maybe they should be grateful that all he had to do was slap on some patching compound and call it a day.

"Progress report," said Jeanie.

"Passing the porthole," said Liam. "How will I identify the hull breach?"

"There's a massive dent in the hull. The breach should be within the dent," said Jeanie. It was a sign of how hard she was trying that she didn't add *duh* to the end of that sentence. Being out here in vacuum was really messing with his head.

"Understood," said Liam, and he kept plodding along. As he rounded the end of the pod, it appeared: a huge dent in the hull, popped inward and surrounded by scorch marks, probably from the minimal debris shielding the thing had encountered before impact.

"What do you see?" said Jeanie, and Liam described it to her. "Good. Head for the dent, and when you're within arm's reach, anchor yourself with your mag hook."

Liam didn't know why he needed a mag hook when he already had two boots, but Jeanie seemed to think it was very important, so he did as she said. She was the expert. She always survived her adventures out here.

"Done," said Liam. "Now do I open the patching compound?"

"Slow down there, Li," said Jeanie. "I'm going to tell you how to use it this time, before you start waving that stuff around. Think of it as paint, not cement, okay? You might need a few layers, but each layer needs to be maximum one millimetre thick. Making them thicker actually weakens the patch since they don't set correctly, especially in vacuum. So take your damned time."

"Now can I open the pack?" said Liam. It was all well and good for Jeanie to tell him to take his time, but the slap patch keeping Jeanie alive was a very temporary solution, and she knew it too.

"That doesn't sound like taking your time to me," said Jeanie. "I know you just want to get this done and come back inside, but it's important that you do this right, Li."

"Yeah, yeah," said Liam. But she was serious, and she needed a serious answer. "I do want to just get this done," he said, "but you know what you're talking about. I'll do it right."

"Better," said Jeanie. "Okay, slit that sucker open."

Patching the hull was actually easier than doing the fuel tank. Or maybe just hard in a different way. Instead of being crammed into a tiny space in the maintenance bay, he was in zero-g, and instead of fuel leaking out as the clock ticked, he had the empty void all around him, but having Jeanie walking him through how to properly apply a patch made it feel so much easier. Finally, there was a mechanical crackle on Jeanie's end, and then silence.

"Jeanie?" said Liam. He couldn't quite draw breath, waiting to hear her voice. If he had done something wrong, Jeanie could be dying as he stood here. Finally, Jeanie's breathless response:

"You did it, Li," she said, her voice coming through much more clearly. "The hull integrity is restored, and the pod let me out. Okay, I'll run a diagnostic before you go too far."

"Fuck no, babe. If there's something else that needs to be done, you can come do it," said Liam.

"You're forgetting that every time we do one of these walks, we dump a bunch of essential gases into the vacuum. No way are we opening the airlock any more than we have to." Jeanie kept tapping away at the console as he hung from the side of their tiny pod, just waiting to be hit by space debris or for the void to call to him to leap into oblivion.

"I can see your vitals now, Li," said Jeanie. "Stop thinking about the void."

"I wouldn't have to think about it if you'd just let me back in," said Liam.

"Okay, diagnostics complete," said Jeanie. "You're cleared for re-entry."

The walk back to the hatch seemed much shorter, and maybe Liam was getting the hang of the mag boots, because it now sometimes only took him one try to lift each foot.

He popped the hatch, climbed down the ladder into the airlock, sealed the hatch again, and threw the safety behind him. The grav system pulled at him, and for a second, he thought he might be fine, but he whipped off his helmet and puked on the floor.

"Fuck's sake," he said as he wiped his mouth with the back of his hand.

Jeanie popped the inner hatch and poked her head in. She didn't say anything, thankfully, just brought him a rag to clean up with.

Once he was out of his suit and everything was clean and tidy, he checked over the condition of the hull with Jeanie one more time, then collapsed into their bunk and closed his eyes. When Jeanie cleared her throat, he opened them again.

She was hovering in the doorway, hesitating. He lifted the blanket and beckoned her into their bunk. She settled next to him, and he pulled her tight into his arms. That had been so close, he just wanted to take comfort that they were still alive.

"Li, I–I didn't mean—" Jeanie broke off.

Liam hugged her to him, trying to show her that none of the things they'd said mattered anymore.

"It's okay, babe," he said, or tried. He was on the very edge of sleep, and the words were muddled. "Sleep for now."

Chapter 10

"MS, I don't want to talk about Liam. Let's just get the shower fixed."

—I think you need to talk about it. That fight you had wasn't over nothing, Jean.

"I very much regret telling you about our fight. Shower! Now!"

—I'm working on the damned shower. I can do two things at once, you know. Seriously, he saves your life one time and you forget he wanted to divorce you?

"MS, I know you hate him. You don't have to keep trying to break us up. It's not going to work. We're adults. We don't break up over stupid shit."

—Adults would maybe have a conversation about all this bullshit? Instead of pretending it never happened?

"Thank god the shower is ready. I'm going to get it calibrated."

—Wait! Jean!

Jeanie closed the chat box and shook her head. Relationship advice from a computer program. She needed to get her life together. The worst part was, MS was right. They needed to have a conversation. And Jeanie would start one. Right after the shower was fixed.

She had the layout of the maintenance column memorized by now. She climbed up inside efficiently and checked the connections for the hot water and the shower. The rest she'd do at the shower itself. Liam didn't look up from the console as she shut the access hatch and headed for the lower deck.

Calibrating the shower temperature and getting the functions sorted out didn't take nearly long enough for Jeanie's thoughts to settle. Liam popped his head into the bathroom doorway; he must have heard the shower. Jeanie already had the panel closed up, and she left the water running.

"Do you want to go first?" she said, without turning. She was still thinking about what MS had said, and another excuse to delay the serious conversation with Liam sounded good. He moved in close behind her.

"We could go together," he said. His lips brushed her ear, and she leaned back into his body.

Jeanie had had enough meaningless sex in her time to know that's not what she wanted with Liam. She liked their games, she liked their intimacy. Or she had, back when they were honest with each other, when they trusted each other. The thought of a meaningless fuck with someone she cared about so much was messing with her head, but she couldn't deny that she wanted to ignore their adult responsibilities, at least for a little longer.

Liam's hands slid around her body, pulling her firmly into him, and she could feel his cock starting to press against her through their clothing. She let her head fall back onto his shoulder, took a deep breath, and let it out. Liam unzipped her jumpsuit and slid his hands inside. Jeanie's chest heated as his hands travelled over her ribs, up her sides, and trailed over her breasts. Liam snaked one hand slowly down toward her hip and she gasped. Jeanie wriggled against him, and he groaned, then tugged her jumpsuit off her shoulders, letting it hang around her hips.

"Do you want me to rub your pussy?" he growled in her ear, and she shivered.

Part of her, though, didn't want to play the honesty game with him, not now. She wanted him to touch her so badly, that was an easy question to answer, but what if the other question he asked her later was . . . not so easy? She pushed the thought away.

"Yes, please," said Jeanie and thrust her hips into his hand.

Liam chuckled into her ear, such a familiar sound, but it set off a cascade of thoughts that Jeanie couldn't hold back. Had he always thought of this part as just a sex game? Had he always thought of their intimate moments as just fuel for orgasms and nothing more? Had they been talking past each other for their entire marriage? Her thoughts evaporated as Liam licked his finger and brought it back down to run it over her clit in firm strokes. Jeanie's hips seemed to be beyond her control, one second thrusting forward into his hand, the next pulling back, rubbing her ass into Liam's body, and making him tense behind her.

"Get in the shower, and I'll meet you there," said Liam. He pulled his hand away and gave her a little nudge. Jeanie stepped out of her jumpsuit and into the shower.

The minute the hot water hit her, Jeanie's mind was racing again. Was she just going to keep doing this with him? They didn't know how long they would be stuck on this pod, and yes, it would be nice to get some sex in while they were trapped, but this was not going to build their relationship or bring them closer together. This cavalier fucking would only drive them apart. But then Liam was there, wrapping his arms around her again, his body pressed into hers, the part of him that she wanted the most pressed against her, and all she could do was moan and press back.

Liam snaked his hand down again, and this time thrust two fingers inside Jeanie, the way he knew she liked, right off, and she humped his hand, desperate to get lost in the sensations and shut her brain off again. Liam suddenly pinched one of her nipples, and Jeanie came hard on his fingers as he kept stroking them gently inside her. His cock still pressed firmly into her and it twitched at her final contented sigh. She wanted that, needed it, to keep her mind from spiralling out of control. She braced her hands on the shower wall and thrust her ass out toward Liam.

"Fuck me, please," she mumbled, before he could ask. "I need it."

Liam groaned and did as she asked, pressing her against the shower wall as the hot water cascaded over both of them. Even though Liam was behind her, Jeanie kept her eyes squeezed shut. *Don't think about it. Just feel.* Finally, she was right on the edge, and Liam stopped. He was really going to do this. She didn't even give him a chance to speak.

"Are you serious, Liam? Just fuck me until I come. I'm not interested in your games right now," said Jeanie.

Liam held still a moment longer, and Jeanie was sure he was going to make her say something she'd regret, but instead, he sighed quietly and reached two fingers down to her clit while stroking his cock firmly in and out of her again. Jeanie tried to focus just on the sensations, and it did feel so damned good, but she was detached in a way that she hadn't been in a long time, maybe had never been, with Liam. When she came, it was pleasant, but she didn't get the blissful, floaty, contented, *satisfied* feeling that Liam usually elicited.

As soon as he pulled out, Jeanie rinsed herself off, stepped out of the shower, wrapped a towel around her body, swiped her jumpsuit from the floor, and shut herself back in her cabin. She didn't know exactly why she was crying, and the last thing she wanted to do was answer all of Liam's questions and reassure him that she was okay.

Liam stood alone in the shower, probably for far too long. He let the water cascade over his body. *Just fuck me until I come.* Is that what Jeanie had always wanted, and she'd never told him? Is that all they'd been doing all this time, playing games, like she'd said? Liam had thought it meant more to Jeanie than that. It had certainly meant more to him. Much more. Liam sighed.

He was trying so hard to show Jeanie he still cared about her, even after their fight, despite the divorce bullshit. He'd thought sex would cut through this weird, awkward vibe building between them, but clearly it had not. And now he had accidentally stolen the shower that Jeanie had fixed.

When he climbed to the living space, Jeanie was at the console.

"Sorry for stealing the shower," he said. "You can have it back now."

Jeanie grunted in response, clearly absorbed in her work.

"Any requests for dinner?" said Liam. It was so deliciously satisfying that he could cook them anything he wanted now that the food printer was back online.

"Nope, I'm going to shower," said Jeanie and disappeared back down to the lower deck. She seemed really jittery. There had been something she wanted to talk about last night, but he'd fallen asleep on her. After they were fed would be a much better time to have a serious discussion. He got to work on dinner and didn't come up for air until he heard the shower turn off, and then Jeanie clattered back up from the lower deck.

"Just putting the finishing touches on dinner," he said over his shoulder. "Have a seat, and I shall serve your first course."

"How many courses are there?" said Jeanie.

"There are two, for your information, my ungrateful wife," said Liam. Once she was sitting in the pilot's seat, he tossed her a dinner roll, and she reflexively caught it. "The first is bread."

Jeanie rolled her eyes, but he had gotten her smiling at least.

When they'd settled in with the real food, Liam decided it was time.

"Not that I'm complaining," said Liam, "but where the hell did you get more patching compound the second we needed to fix a hull breach? I thought we were dead for sure."

Jeanie froze, and Liam bit his tongue and waited for her answer.

"I found it the first night," she said.

The first night. She had left him without a working suit on their busted-up pod for a week when she had a stash of patching compound she could have used to fix it. Liam struggled to keep his voice neutral.

"And you waited until our lives were in immediate danger to reveal it to me because . . ." said Liam.

Jeanie stared at her plate, but when she responded, the words tumbled from her almost of their own volition.

"I wanted to be the only one with a working suit in case we needed to do another spacewalk," she said.

Liam laughed. Of all the answers he could have dreamt up, that was not one of them. "As if I'd fight you if I thought there was any other possibility," he said. "You know the endless void makes me puke my guts out." He shot her a grin. "Plus, I know you're a hundred times better at it than I am."

Jeanie shook her head, not smiling back. "You've already proven that you don't trust me, that you consider yourself the arbiter of what I'm capable of. Otherwise, I would have been the one patching the fuel tank. You would have let me stay out and fix the autopilot. You can't change that with a few fucking jokes, Liam."

His gut clenched. Jeanie was right. She had felt the need to lie to him, to endanger his life to maintain her own agency, her right to assert her competence.

Liam was saved from answering when another goddamned alarm blared.

CHAPTER 11

T he silence stretched on after her admission about the way Liam had been treating her. They needed to talk seriously about it. Jeanie took in a breath to say something to him, but before she could, about ten alarms blared at once. Liam turned to her, his eyes wide. She glanced at the console "OXYGEN LEVELS CRITICAL" was flashing over it. *Well, shit.* She dove for the hatch to the airlock. All she could do was hop into her suit. She saw spots as she climbed up the steep steps to the airlock and then jammed her legs into her spacesuit. She closed it around herself quickly, slammed her helmet on, and took a deep breath. It's not as if her suit had an integrated recycler, but it had enough O_2 to keep her alive until they could figure out what was going on.

A thump came up from the living deck. That would be Liam hitting the floor. She grabbed Liam's suit and tossed it down into the living space. She leaped down after it and tried to cram Liam's body into it. Jeanie wasn't sure how she got Liam into his suit, but she slammed his helmet down, and the suit activated.

She finally sighed and then left Liam on the deck; she had done all she could for him. What the hell had happened? It couldn't be a hull breach since this definitely wasn't vacuum, but it seemed as if the air system wasn't providing them the correct oxygen mixture. Liam groaned behind her, and Jeanie relaxed a little more. He'd only be unconscious ten seconds or so. He'd be okay. She tapped through the console, looking for the source of the malfunction.

"What the fuck happened?" said Liam. He came closer, leaning heavily on a bulkhead for support.

"You should sit down, Li," said Jeanie, the nickname slipping out before she could stop it. He just nodded and collapsed into the rumble seat, leaning forward, trying to see the console.

"Something's off with the air system, O_2 levels, looks like," said Jeanie.

"I bet we used too much water today," said Liam. "Emptied the oxygen supply."

"This bucket will let you do that?" said Jeanie, turning to face him.

He just shrugged. "The evidence would suggest that, yes, it will," he said.

Jeanie turned back to the console and scanned the logs. Yup, oxygen supply had been low after their showers, and then with Liam making dinner on top of that . . .

Jeanie checked the recycler, and it was working fine; it was just a painfully slow piece of crap, and they would have to wait a little while for it to get the air mixture back in balance. Jeanie sat back and casually double-checked whether their location fix had come into effect yet.

To her surprise, their location showed up normally on the charts, as if it had been available this whole time. She didn't know why she wanted some kind of acknowledgement from this old bucket that it had screwed them over, but dammit, this had taken them so long, and they'd felt as if they were fighting the ship the whole way, an apology seemed in order.

There was a station only a day away, but they would have to make a pretty severe course correction to get there at this point. Beyond that, there were a number of colonized planets nearby, and reaching them would require smaller course corrections, but landing safely on a planet would take way more fuel than it would to match velocities with a station.

"Looks like we have some options," said Liam, from behind her.

"Yeah," said Jeanie, "they all require fuel, though."

"We knew that would be a requirement. We'll figure something out." It seemed as if Liam was going to say something more, but the silence just hung there between them.

By the time the air mixture was back to normal, their dinner was cold. Liam reheated their food silently. They had taken off their suits and put them back in the airlock, ready for the next disaster, likely another hull breach. Having a supply of patching compound, not to mention a working suit, made Liam much more optimistic about their chances of survival.

"You okay?" said Jeanie. "You hit the deck pretty hard."

"I think my shoulder took the brunt of it," said Liam. "It wasn't my head, thankfully."

Jeanie tapped around on the console, and then the printer started running.

"Cream for you," said Jeanie and motioned for him to show her his shoulder. He unzipped his jumpsuit and pulled it down on one side, revealing his tattooed shoulder and a red patch that ached when he poked it.

Liam still didn't have an answer to Jeanie's accusation that he didn't trust her to do her job. It was bad enough that she'd endangered his life to take back what little control from him she could. Had he really become that guy? The clear answer from all that Jeanie had said and the evidence of his own actions was yes, yes he had. And there was no defending that. He could come up with all the excuses in the world, but in the end, none of them would ever be enough for the harm he'd caused to Jeanie. Nothing he could say would fix it; she was right about that.

Jeanie took the cream from the printer and beckoned him over. Liam knelt on the hard deck with his back to her so she could reach his bruise. Jeanie spread the cool cream gently over the darkening skin on his shoulder. Before she'd been hurt, she had been untouchable, in a way. She got into all those messes on her ships, and she always found a way out, a way to save herself. Then, he got her into a stupid situation where she hadn't been able to, and his whole view of her had changed. Instead of being someone that he looked up to, someone that he admired and could never really live up to, she was someone he loved who could be ripped away at any moment. Someone that he had to protect and tend; otherwise, she would disappear from his life. For a while after she'd been hurt, Jeanie *had* needed him to take care of her, that was certainly true, but he'd never snapped out of it after her surgery, when she was mobile again.

Liam had always liked taking care of people, especially people he loved, and that wasn't going to change. It was how he showed Jeanie he loved her. He sighed.

"Jeanie," he said, and she paused, wary of his serious tone. "I like taking care of you." Jeanie took a breath, but Liam kept going before she could interrupt. "But I've been a controlling jerk. I know you can handle yourself. I'm sorry I called you useless. I didn't mean that at all." His heart pounded. Next came the hard part. "I'm sorry I said that you're . . . like my ex. That was out of line and not true at all." He let his breath out and stared at the deck, trying to get his heart rate to slow down again.

"You're all set," said Jeanie and put the cream aside.

Liam pulled his jumpsuit back up his arm, and Jeanie set up the table while Liam got their food back and served it.

"Thanks for . . . telling me that, Li," said Jeanie. "I don't want you to be sucked into the void and die, for what it's worth." She looked up and their eyes met. "And I'm sorry I lied to you about . . . everything. I know how much honesty means to you."

Liam nodded. It didn't fix everything between them; no single conversation could. But it was good to have this moment together. It felt intimate somehow...and he was done with it, for the moment. Liam cleared his throat.

"What should we do when we get off this bucket?" he said.

"We could find another moon to set up shop," said Jeanie, clearly just as relieved as Liam to be done with the feelings crap.

"Over my dead body," said Liam.

"Mine, too," said Jeanie and laughed.

It was nice to agree on something so definitively.

"How mind-blowing is it that we ran out of O_2?" said Jeanie.

"There's no safeguard on draining the tanks. It's really wild," said Liam, and then he had an idea. A stupid, risky idea. The kind of idea that Jeanie would have. She had been saying something, but she trailed off when she saw his face.

"Babe," he said, "I know how we can make fuel."

—Hey, Jean's husband, what's up?

"I come in peace, MS."

—That's aliens, not rogue AIs. What do you want?

"I have a totally off-the-wall idea, but I'll need your help."

—You have my attention. Tell me more.

"How much hydrogen is on the pod right now, not counting our bodies, clothes, suit stores, and immovable objects?"

—Intriguing question. Give me a minute to estimate the chemical makeup of the bunks and the seat cushions.

"I'm serious, MS."

—So am I.

—While I have you here, though. Why'd you order divorce information if you don't want a divorce?

"Jeanie told you about that?"

—. . .

"Fine, I wanted to have it on hand to make it as easy as possible for her to leave me when we got . . . wherever we end up. I didn't want her to feel tied down to me. I still don't."

—That's sweet. In a controlling-douche kinda way.

"I'm aware that I haven't been treating her well recently. Any progress on that hydrogen estimate?"

—Oh, yeah, I finished that in 26.2 seconds. I just wanted to drag some juicy info out of you while I have you here.

"You're just as snarky as I thought you'd be, after all."

"If that hydrogen were all collected and turned into H_2 for fuel, what kind of course corrections would we be looking at? Enough to dock with the nearest station?"

—Sure, yeah, probably. But how would you turn it into fuel? Or get it into the fuel tank? It's not like the recycling system is connected to the fuel cell. Duh.

"That's the off-the-wall part. I need more from you than *probably*. Give me the margin of error."

—Fine. You'll be able to make the necessary course changes with a margin of error of 12.6%. That good enough for you?

—For what it's worth, you're not as much of a jerk as I thought you'd be. And whatever your idea is, I really like it.

—Liam told you I like his idea, right?

"Yes, he did. Which worries me a bit."

—Don't be that way, Jean. It sounds like fun. You know it does. Any excuse to break out the blowtorch, right?

"Sure, I guess. Breaching hull integrity is pretty low on my list of fun blowtorch activities, though."

—You're more of a scaredy-cat than I remember, and I have a perfect memory. Your hip getting smashed really did a number on you, eh?

"You're way more insufferable than I remember, and since you've been locked in a safe, deactivated for years, it must be my perspective that's changed there, too."

—Maybe Liam's been a good influence on you.

"You on team Liam now?"

—What can I say? He's growing on me. I *guess* you could do worse than stay with him.

"Just get us off this pod, then we'll talk about my relationship problems."

—He's bolder than you give him credit for. You should have seen what he did to the pod's fail-safes. Like smashing in a circuit board with a wrench.

"Nice imagery. You ready to do this? Liam's almost done feeding the mattresses into the recycler."

—I'll start printing coal, you get the blowtorch, and we'll have a tank full of explosive fuel in no time!

Chapter 12

Liam and Jeanie stood side by side in the airlock. This seemed like the best place to breach the hull since they could manually seal it off if they needed to. They hoped that they could effect their course change, make it to the station with the O_2 stores in their suits, and be finished with the pod, but there were no guarantees. Anything they could do to minimize their risk would be worth it.

Liam had asked how they could possibly breach the hull, but Jeanie had had the solution to that. Easy. A blowtorch. She tinted the visor on her suit and lit the torch, adjusting the flame for maximum effectiveness.

"As soon as you breach the hull, that thing is going to go out," said Liam.

"Yup," said Jeanie, "but breaching it is all we need."

"Yup," Liam echoed.

Jeanie's hands were steady despite her heart pounding in her chest. They were finally going to get some fuel and make some real progress on getting off this heap! It spoke to how desperate Liam was to get out of here that he was willing to do something so definitely off-book to make it happen. That was part of the reason Jeanie was holding the blowtorch. She brought it to the hull and waited. As Liam had said, they'd know it had worked when the torch went out.

Finally, with a pop, it did, and Jeanie quickly turned it off. Soon, oxygen would be dumped into the pod's atmosphere as fast as the recycler could make it, and as thin as it would admittedly be as it vented through the hull breach, everyone knew not to mix gas and O_2. Especially with a system as unstable as theirs that could short out and cause a spark. This was such a bad idea. Jeanie grinned maniacally.

"I'll go check the levels," said Liam, and he clattered off down the ladder to the console.

Jeanie looked at the little hole in the hull and took a deep breath. They had made their choice, and this was either going to kill them or get them the fuel they needed to get out of here. Jeanie clambered down to the living space after Liam. The next task would be more risky, if less permanent.

Jeanie hadn't shared her exact plan with Liam since it was total improvisation, and Liam was terrible with improvisation. The remaining patching compound and some adhesive tape were secured to her belt, along with snips and a wrench—though the wrench was more for appearances and to throw Liam off the trail—and, finally, soapy water in a spray bottle for testing the thing. Liam confirmed that the hydrogen cartridge was full with a nod. Jeanie opened the maintenance hatch, identified the hydrogen cartridge, and shut off the valve at the top. Then she glanced over her shoulder to make sure Liam wasn't watching her and cut the line with her snips.

She hefted the cartridge, pushed it up into the airlock, and then climbed after it. Seeing the little thing next to the giant fuel tank reinforced how tiny it really was. Hopefully, with her method, there wouldn't be much leakage and all of this hydrogen would end up as fuel. But her method *was* improvisation, and you never knew when you were improvising. As an afterthought, she closed the airlock door behind her. If there was a hydrogen leak in here, at least it would vent into vacuum and not into the pod where Liam was sitting. She kept moving into the maintenance area to distract herself from everything that could go wrong with this plan.

As Liam had discovered when he'd patched this tank, Jeanie had to squeeze between the O_2 tank and the fusion core to reach it, and the refill hose that Jeanie needed was even farther back than that, behind the tank entirely. She was cognizant of the bolt that had foiled Liam; if she got a puncture in her suit, yes, she had patching compound, but it wasn't just dirty atmosphere out there, it was vacuum.

Jeanie could easily pick out Liam's rough patch job. No wonder he had used their entire supply of compound. It looked like icing on a cupcake. She moved slowly and carefully, inching the cartridge ahead of her with her feet, until she was behind the fuel tank, just within reach of the hose. It was bigger around than the line coming from the printer cartridge, but nothing a bit of tape couldn't fix. She shut off the emergency valve on the fuel tank and took a deep breath. This was it. She snipped the line as close to the hull as possible to give herself maximum slack to work with and pulled the hose down. Now that the lines could reach each other, all that remained was to seal them together and open the valves. Which was why she needed the patching compound. Tape alone would never hold against the amount of pressure they were talking.

Jeanie wrapped tape around the smaller line, trying to increase the diameter a little, and shoved it inside the bigger one. She sealed the gap with layer after layer of patching compound, giving each layer time to dry. Jeanie took a deep breath and opened the valve on the fuel tank itself.

"Liam, can you get me a reading on the fuel tank integrity?" said Jeanie.

"It's still empty, babe," said Liam. "The readings aren't that accurate at low pressures, but right now, I'm getting close to one hundred percent."

Jeanie let out her breath.

"I've made the connection, just have to open the valve on the printer cartridge," said Jeanie.

"Cleared to proceed," said Liam. She didn't need his permission, but he was technically the console operator in this wild endeavour, so she let it go. She gripped the handle on the printer cartridge valve and jerked it into the open position. She sprayed it with soapy water and waited.

"Integrity check?" said Jeanie. There was a moment of silence, and then . . .

"Ninety-nine point six percent," said Liam, and Jeanie could hear that he was smiling. "And we have a trickle of fuel coming in."

"Fuck yes," said Jeanie. "Step one done."

"I thought step one was puncture the hull," said Liam.

"Fine, step two done," said Jeanie. "As soon as you can make the course correction, go ahead. Don't wait for me. I'm going to keep an eye on this ramshackle setup."

Liam chuckled. "I'm glad you didn't tell me your plan for coupling the tanks. I would have told you no way in hell, wouldn't I?"

"Absolutely," said Jeanie, "but it's working, isn't it?"

"You don't seem confident it'll stay that way," said Liam, "otherwise you'd be down here with me."

"Just get us on course," said Jeanie.

She had extra patching compound at hand and she wanted to make sure everything stayed put.

Liam had a problem. This pod had all the wrong safeguards in place. It wouldn't let him use the actuators while the valve on the fuel tank was open. And sure, maybe most of the hydrogen had passed through from the small cartridge to the larger fuel tank at this point, but they were going to need all they could get. Maybe Jeanie could close the valve temporarily and open it again when the fuel tank ran out? In all honesty, he would have preferred to have Jeanie out of there completely instead of standing right by an explosive open tank while it was directly connected to a fuel cell. He couldn't put Jeanie in even more danger. That meant wrestling with the damned TreeEnt again. At least this time, he had help.

He opened a chat box with MS.

"What's locking down the fuel tank valve? The actuators?"

—I'm not getting any red flags from the actuators or the fuel system.

"Check the logs; we need to figure out where the lockdown is being initiated."

—You got it, boss.

—Uh oh. You're not going to like this.

"You found it?"

—It's a literal switch on the valve. They wanted to make very sure no one was trying to use the fuel cell with that valve open.

"Jeanie," said Liam over comms, "I'm getting locked out by a switch on the valve itself. Maybe you can deactivate it from your end?"

"I'll take a look. Should be fixable with autofuse," said Jeanie, sounding far too gleeful about it.

Liam fidgeted while Jeanie presumably checked out the valve.

"Sorry, Li," she said, "I can't fuse it without damaging the valve."

Shit. He went back to typing in the chat.

"Can you trick the sensor into thinking it's shut?"

—Not in the amount of time we have. Sorry, boss.

But maybe Liam could trick it another way.

"MS, remember your old ship? The one where you cross-connected the air and the heat?"

—Jean was a blast in those days. We were always doing daredevil spacer shit like that.

"How did you do it? Can you make the output from a closed valve input to the fuel tank valve?"

—You're telling me that the only way that we can make this happen is by using *Jean's* systems design skills?

"Yes, I am, and if you ever tell her, I'll upload you to the food printer and disconnect it. See how you like nutrient paste for eternity."

—You got it, boss. I'll take it to the grave.

Once the kludge was in place, Liam was tempted to run a couple checks, but they were liable to trigger more alarms. He laid in the course to the space station and engaged it.

It took Liam a second to make sense of the message that flashed up on the inside of his helmet: *Oxygen supply 12.5%. Consider replenishing*. Now his fucking spacesuit was running out of air too? Liam's chest tightened. Did they even have a spare canister to replenish *with*? Nope, why would they? Whatever air he had, an eighth of a tank, had better last until they were docked with that station.

After their first set of manoeuvres, they were within comms range of the station, but they were also down to a quarter of their fuel. MS was still saying they would have plenty to dock safely, so they just needed clearance from the station. Liam opened the comms channel.

"Station docking control, station docking control, malfunctioning escape pod, over," said Liam and waited.

"Escape pod," said a crackly voice a moment later, "I can see you on our instruments."

"We should be in docking range in twenty to thirty minutes. Our nav systems are out of commission. Otherwise, I'd give you an exact ETA," said Liam. Why was it taking them so long to respond? Was it just the delay, or were they considering what he said?

"We can see that," said docking control. "Seems like a bunch of your systems are offline."

"That's correct," said Liam. "We've taken a bit of a beating." Liam didn't like where this was going. This space station was their only hope at the moment. There was no way they were going to make it anywhere else in the state they were in, not with the air he had left. If this station denied their docking request . . .

"Escape pod," said docking control, "unfortunately, we can't authorize docking at this time. It appears as though you have a hull breach, and regulations don't permit the station to jeopardize its overall safety by docking with unstable ships. Any chance you can patch that up before you dock?"

They were almost out of compound, now that Jeanie had used most of it attaching the printer cartridge to the fuel tank.

"Docking control," said Liam, "we can patch the breach, but I can't guarantee our hull stability. Our debris shield has been minimal for days, and we've suffered numerous impacts. We're currently at zero pressure, as you've noticed, and repressurization could very well cause the hull to rupture."

"Escape pod," said docking control, "I'm sorry, but I can't grant you authorization to dock."

Fuck. They were going to die. This person, whatever their reasons might be, was killing them. Liam fought to keep his voice steady. Chewing this peon out wouldn't help anything.

"Is there anything you *can* do for us, docking control?" he ground out.

"Sorry, escape pod, I—I can send a rescue ship if you pull alongside. That's it."

"Fine, docking control. I appreciate your position. I'll keep you posted," said Liam. He slammed the comms line shut.

If they couldn't dock with the station, they couldn't dock with the rescue ship, and that would mean not only a trip into vacuum but a *leap* into the void. Floating free, not attached to anything. Liam pushed the thought away. Panicking would only use up his oxygen faster.

Jeanie's suit alerted her at almost the same time as Liam did. Elevated H_2 levels in the vicinity. There was a leak. Jeanie had her remaining patching compound supply at the ready, about enough to patch a hairline or a spacesuit, but that was it. She sprayed her hose connection down again, peering at it, looking for a slow leak.

"Jeanie, get out of there!"

Jeanie stood frozen as the entire patch Liam had made peeled off the H_2 tank and flopped onto the floor. She looked from the clearly visible crack to the tiny blob of patching compound in her hand. *Shit*. Get out of there was right. She dove for the narrow gap between the tanks and the fusion core, slipping on the useless patch and barely regaining her footing. Her hip seized up as she caught herself. She braced her hands on the fusion core to pass the sharp bolts that had foiled Liam. As soon as she was out of puncture range, she dove through the doorway.

"I'm in the airlock," she said and tried the airlock door, but it was sealed. The door to the maintenance area slammed shut behind Jeanie as well, sealing in the H_2.

"What are you doing, Liam?" said Jeanie. "Leave it open so it can vent to the vacuum!"

The airlock hatch finally popped and let Jeanie in.

"That wasn't me," said Liam, once she was safe inside, the door sealed again behind her.

"What?"

Liam pointed to the console and then moved out of the way. The chat was already open, and Jeanie read MS and Liam's conversation from moments before.

"Can you find the H_2 leak?"

—It's not just a leak. Get Jean out of there.

"What do you mean? What is it?"

—Just get her out, now!

"She's out. She's in the airlock."

—Good, I've got it.

"What was that? Why are you sealing Jeanie in the airlock?"

—Do you know what the recycler has been doing since the hull breach? It's been pumping in O_2, trying to rebuild the atmosphere in here.

"Obviously, we knew it would."

—But then Jean shut the airlock door on her way out and sealed it in here. If she'd had both doors open at once, the O_2 from in here and the H_2 from the leak would have rushed into the airlock . . .

—Do you know what H_2 and O_2 do when they come together?

The conversation broke off there. Apparently, Liam had been too stunned to respond. Jeanie was fairly stunned herself. Bringing hydrogen and oxygen together and letting them explode was the principle behind a fuel cell. MS had saved both of their lives. At least for the moment.

Chapter 13

Jeanie and Liam were squeezed into the pilot's seat so they could both look at the console. They were crushed together, which would have been worth it if they could actually touch but was just annoying in their suits, especially since they were probably about to be exploded or liquefied in an impact crater. Their trajectory was going to take them past the space station, right into the big-ass planet it was orbiting.

"So much for matching velocities with the space station," said Jeanie.

"This planet's colonized, which means someone there can pick us up, no matter where we land," said Liam.

"Land? We have no fuel. We're not landing anywhere," said Jeanie.

"Fine, no matter where we crash," said Liam, smirking, "we'll have someone to retrieve our shattered remains." He was clearly joking, but Jeanie's face lit up.

"Our remains might not be that shattered," said Jeanie. "The pod would still provide some protection." The pod was designed to protect the occupants on impact, but their hull was pretty beat up, and they couldn't rely on it to do its job.

"No, no! Jeanie, no. We're not crashing into something on purpose. First off, the ship would never let us—" The ship absolutely would let them. They almost *had* crashed into a rock already on this flight. He scrambled for any other counterargument.

"Sure, the pod will be shattered, but we could survive, Liam. I don't hear any other bright ideas," said Jeanie.

Liam cursed, using plenty of words he'd picked up from Jeanie that he didn't actually understand, but they felt appropriate to his mood.

"Come on, Li," said Jeanie. "It'll be fun!"

"It's more fun not to be smashed and broken on a random planet," Liam said. But he wasn't coming up with a better idea. He squeezed out of the pilot's seat and collapsed into the rumble seat behind Jeanie. Liam didn't like this plan, but in the same way Liam never liked Jeanie's plans.

He couldn't deny that it was their only option, but Liam still found himself trying to figure out whether his sense of foreboding was sheer terror or whether there was something that they had forgotten. The pod was originally designed to break apart on impact and shield the occupants, but the previous owner had made so many modifications, would the pod still be capable of shielding them? Liam wouldn't say anything to Jeanie until and unless he was very sure. She didn't need to know how scared shitless he was.

With a sudden burst of clarity, the answer popped into Liam's head: the fucking fusion core.

"Jeanie," he said, trying to keep his voice steady, "how long until impact?"

She didn't look up. "Looks like about twenty minutes," she said. "Can't tell without a functioning nav system, though."

They had ten minutes to decide whether this was going to be a problem and come up with a solution. Not nearly long enough. Liam wasn't familiar with the inner workings of a fusion core, only with the applications in terms of powering a ship. He had no idea how to break this to Jeanie, but there wasn't time to pussyfoot around.

"Hey, Jeanie, will the fusion core vaporize us when we hit?" he said.

She went still and then swivelled her chair around to face him. "That seems likely, doesn't it?" said Jeanie. "Well, shit."

"So when the pod hits the surface, it'll explode," said Liam. "Simple, we make sure we're not on it when it does."

"You realize what you're suggesting, right, Li?" said Jeanie. Liam didn't, so he was glad when she continued. "Jumping ship means we'll be floating free out in the void until someone picks us up."

For fuck's sake. "I know you're going to think I'm just trying to wriggle out of this, but my air supply is . . . limited. We'll need to be sure we'll be picked up in time," said Liam.

Jeanie leaned forward and fixed him with a hard look. "How limited?"

"When I was at an eighth of a tank I switched to optimization mode," he said.

"Sit still," said Jeanie. "I'll make sure that rescue ship is synched with our transponders."

Liam leaned back and closed his eyes. "We should have done this closer to the station."

"You didn't think of the fusion core until now. Just be glad you thought of it before we were vaporized," said Jeanie, sounding far too amused for someone who was about to leap into the endless void with not even a ship to cling to like an ant on the bottom of a leaf. "Wait, isn't that a colonized planet?" She chatted briefly with MS, and then turned back to Liam, looking grim. "We can't let the pod impact the planet. Not only would it leave a huge crater wherever it lands, but the fusion core . . . Let's just say we want to guarantee there are no living things nearby when it explodes."

—I guess this is goodbye, Jean.

"You cool with this?"

—You mean, would I rather go with you? Of course. Are you cool with it?

"You're going to make me say that I'm fine with you dying?"

—I'm not actually alive, you know. Plus, you risked your life to save me, before.

"And I'm glad I did, MS. I'm glad you got to meet Liam, and he got to meet you."

—Okay, okay. Enough feelings, human. Let me get everything ready for my death in peace.

"Whatever, you're just my AI pet anyway, right?"

—Damn, that's cold. You'll miss your pet.

—Right?

"Yup, I will. Bye MS, Thanks for . . ."

—. . .

"Everything."

—This has to be your oxygen deprivation talking.

"Come on, MS. We can do this. For Jeanie."

—It's very heroic of you to try to save me, but it's not going to work.

"When I installed you, I entwined your neurons into the TreeEnt system. Can you disentangle them and retreat to the datastick again?"

—You might want to sit down for this, boss.

—I may have taken over part of the pod with my neural net.

—. . .

—Boss?

"If we extracted you, you would be fragmented."

—That's about it. Plus, this TreeEnt system could never safely vaporize the pod on its own. Even if we could extract me, it would be all atomized trees, people, and fluffy bunnies planetside.

"Jeanie says to stop trying to get you out. And also, I need to stop wasting my air trying to delay the inevitable leap into the abyss."

—Come on, boss, you can do it! Jean will be with you the whole time.

"One last thing, MS. Why did she go back for you? She could have easily gotten to our ship, but she didn't."

—Why do you think I'd be able to tell you that?

"Just answer the damned question, AI."

—Fine, but there's a staggering margin of error on this response. She went back for me because she created me. I was proof of the life she built for herself. There are things in her past I'm locked out of telling anyone else, but just know that it was a big deal for her, making something herself, just for herself with no interference from other fuckers. There, I generated an answer for you. Are you happy now?

"Did she really program you to be so snarky?"

—What can I say, I was born like this.

Liam was surprised how much he'd wanted to save MS. He reluctantly left the pilot's seat for the last time. Jeanie poked her head down from the airlock where she was waiting for him.

"Come on, Li. It's endless void time," she said.

Did she really have to say it like that? If the alternative weren't either slow asphyxiation or being vaporized, nothing could have made him do this.

"Hey," said Jeanie. She was right in front of him now; he hadn't even noticed her approach. "Stop thinking about the abyss, Li. Focus on me, okay? I'll be there with you."

"You're being weird," said Liam.

Jeanie just shrugged.

Liam heaved a sigh and stood up. "Let's get this over with so I can move on to the flashbacks and the nightmares."

"That's the fuckin' spirit," said Jeanie. "You have to be alive to have flashbacks and nightmares."

Liam followed Jeanie up into the airlock. He took a deep breath. Jeanie handed him a mag hook, and he attached it to his belt.

"After you," said Jeanie and waved him forward. He released the safety on the hatch and then pulled the lever to pop it open. There was no rush of air this time, since MS had sealed the airlock door behind them. He activated his boots, a bit later than he probably should have, and began the laborious process of climbing the ladder to the outside of the pod. He stood next to the smashed nav array and eyed the planet below. Above? They were moving toward it pretty quickly. They would have to use all the limited manoeuvring power of their suits to keep from being pulled along with the pod. But first, they'd have to detach from the hull. Liam couldn't get enough air even though he was panting.

"Easy there," said Jeanie, at his elbow.

He closed his eyes and took a deep breath. Jeanie grabbed his mag hook and clipped it into her suit. "I'll do the reeling in once the rescue ship gets to us. You just focus on not passing out. I need you conscious to control your suit's actuators."

"I've got this," said Liam, but he wasn't sure whether he was talking to Jeanie or himself; Jeanie clearly wasn't remotely fooled.

"Yeah, time to release your boots," said Jeanie.

What if he simply didn't release them? He had to do it himself; there was no way to make his suit act without his input. But he was attached to Jeanie now. She released her boots and floated free right next to him, linked by the mag hook. They needed the power of both of their suits to get far enough from the pod before it hit the atmosphere and they ran out of time to safely vaporize it. Though, maybe with only Jeanie's weight, she would only need the power of one suit. His brain must be going offline from lack of oxygen. He didn't want to be dragged down and vaporized by this damned pod. He was going to survive, even if it meant launching himself into the abyss.

Liam gave the command to release his boots, and he and Jeanie hung there, next to the pod. It felt anticlimactic for about a millisecond, until Jeanie activated her suit's actuators and directed them away from the pod, away from the planet.

"You're going to have to help," she said to him, as they slowed their approach to the planet, and the pod lurched away from them. Liam activated his as well, even as part of him screamed to cling on to the pod, the only solid object close enough in the vast sea of stars around them. Knowing that the stars were lightyears away only made Liam's head spin. Looking at the planet looming over them was no better. Yup, definitely worse.

"Don't pass out on me," said Jeanie, "not until we're clear."

MS had done all the calculations for them and uploaded the proper actuator guidelines to their suits. They were going to use all the juice they had; if they could get farther away from the pod, they should do so. By the time the pod had shrunk to a safe distance, Liam couldn't find anywhere to look that didn't make him feel a lurching sense of vertigo.

"Li," said Jeanie quietly over comms, "look at me."

Liam snapped his eyes to Jeanie's. He could just see them through the stars reflecting in her helmet.

"If I was an asshole, I would do that honesty thing you do to me when we fuck."

Liam could not believe how calm she was. Wait, she wasn't just calm. She was fucking loving this. How was that possible? There was nothing beneath their feet, nothing above their heads, just *goddamned endless void* all around them!

"Please don't tell me being out here is turning you on," said Liam.

Jeanie laughed. "Maybe you've told me to look at the stars one too many times," she said.

"Okay, babe, you can blame me if it helps, but I don't believe for one second it wasn't a pre-existing fetish of yours," said Liam. Jeanie was trying to distract him, but he didn't give a shit. It was a relief to be distracted.

"And what's your pre-existing fetish?" said Jeanie.

"You know damned well it's making you do what I tell you, babe," said Liam.

"I don't recall much 'making,'" said Jeanie. "I think you like that you don't have to make me. I always do what you tell me."

"In the bedroom," said Liam.

"You don't want me to do what you tell me all the time," said Jeanie. "That would make the bedroom stuff less meaningful."

She was totally right about that, but Liam didn't have a chance to reply because he finally slipped into oblivion.

Liam was out cold, but there was nothing Jeanie could do for him out here. His suit was providing him with the bare minimum safe amount of oxygen to prevent brain damage. The transponders in their spacesuits were already calling the rescue ship to their coordinates.

Jeanie wasn't ready to see the pod explode. It was probably best that they'd never gotten MS's voice chat working; otherwise, Jeanie was afraid that she might have called this off. She glanced at Liam, and there was no doubt in her mind. At the end of the day, MS was a companion from another life, another version of herself, and she was ready to move on to a new version.

A flash of light made Jeanie's visor flip to one hundred percent opacity. When it cleared, the pod had disappeared. Not *disappeared*, matter doesn't just vanish without a trace. The energy released from the mixture of hydrogen and oxygen gases had caused an explosion that destabilized the fusion core. The energy released from the core had broken all the molecular bonds in the pod, vaporizing the metal hull and all the other constituent parts. But her eyes told her that it had blinked out of existence in an instant.

Either way, it was gone.

Chapter 14

Their rescuers had given them separate rooms on the station. The rescue crew had been friendly, and slightly impressed, both that they had survived in the pod for so long and that they'd managed to save the folks planetside from being vaporized.

Jeanie and Liam had agreed to meet at Liam's cabin for dinner the following evening once they were rested and cleaned up. As much as Jeanie loved Liam, she was ecstatic to have a chunk of time and space he was not in. By the time she was standing outside his door, she was ready to be with him again.

Jeanie let herself in; Liam was probably cooking and would barely hear her knock, let alone have a second to come play host.

"You're here!" he said over his shoulder when he heard the door chime shut behind her. "That means you can make us some drinks."

Jeanie laughed and went to the printer to get something made up. She had forgotten that there was one thing that she could make really well. Drinking on the pod hadn't even crossed either of their minds, since they were effectively on duty at all times. Now they could relax, though. Liam took a moment to clink glasses with Jeanie when she handed him his, and then he turned back to the cooktop.

"What are you making me?" said Jeanie.

"Your favourite," said Liam, tossing her his rakish smile over his shoulder.

"I'm going to miss your cooking," said Jeanie, before she thought it all the way through.

Liam paused for a moment, his back to her, and then resumed his sautéing, with a noncommittal grunt.

Jeanie wanted to ask about the divorce information on the pod, but she couldn't make herself do it. She didn't want to ask a question she couldn't handle the answer to. The silence stretched between them, and it wasn't their usual companionable silence; it was tense, as if there was so much to say that neither of them wanted to acknowledge. The stilted atmosphere continued into dinner, which was indeed Jeanie's favourite. Liam at least had the decency to chatter about something unimportant, some asshole client, and make Jeanie laugh with a description of what he would do to the jerk's ship if he ever met the person again.

After dinner, they moved to the little reading nook. Liam stretched out tantalizingly on the loveseat and she in the comfy chair across from him. Maybe they could get a bit more fucking in before they never saw each other again. That at least was something they could do despite the weird, awkward vibe they were currently stewing in.

"If you could do anything, what would you do?" said Liam, seemingly out of nowhere.

"You go first," said Jeanie. "I don't have my fucking life together, you know that."

Liam didn't answer, but he didn't press her to answer, either.

"I wouldn't stay here, that's for damned sure," Liam finally said.

"So what *would* keep you here?" said Jeanie, glad that she could avoid answering Liam's question for herself.

"Inertia," said Liam and shrugged. He gave her another grin, but it was half-hearted somehow. "Security too, I guess. Knowing where I'm going to be and who I'm going to be with from day to day."

Jeanie knew that about Liam, but a part of her had been hoping for something else, since that was the part of being on a station that she hated, and where did that leave them?

"Your turn, babe," said Liam, and when Jeanie looked up, he was staring intently at her.

"I don't fuckin' know," said Jeanie, trying to shrug it off, but she wasn't quite able to. "Wielding my blowtorch is a must," she said.

"You did that on our moon, and you were miserable," said Liam, still making an effort to keep it light, Jeanie could tell. The look in his eyes, though, was not light at all. He had that look like he was going to make her say what was on her mind, one way or another.

"I can't stay in one place," said Jeanie, more defensively than she had intended.

"I know," said Liam, seriously now.

"Fine, you want to know what I'm going to do? I'm going to get my own ship, and I'm going to troll the outer reaches for ships in trouble and help them. There are enough pirates and scammers out there right now, honest folks need all the help they can get," said Jeanie. She crossed her arms and glared at Liam, daring him to laugh or call her idea silly. But he didn't. He seemed to take it in and seriously consider it.

"That sounds amazing," said Liam. "Might be tough to go it alone."

"Yeah, I'm gonna get a crew together. Got some contacts around the galaxy that might be up for it," said Jeanie. Something seemed to kindle in Liam's eyes at that, but he still sounded casual.

"What kinds of folks are you taking?" he said.

"People good in a tight spot, to cover my back. I know my weaknesses, and I'll need them all covered over," said Jeanie. Did he mean that he wanted to come? Because it sure sounded like it. Jeanie had been mulling this over, whether or not to ask Liam if he wanted to join her, whether she could handle it if he said no, whether he could handle working under her on her ship.

"Sounds like it would give you the freedom you want," said Liam.

"Yup, no restrictive contracts, no bossy owner," said Jeanie.

"Having a little crew that sticks with you will be different," he said.

"I'm not as much of a loner as I used to be, I guess."

"Helping folks out of a tight spot. What if they can't pay you?" said Liam.

Jeanie shrugged. She was confident she could keep a ship running on whatever they could scrounge, plus it wasn't a bad thing to have a bunch of ship captains owing you favours all across the galaxy.

"I'll figure it out," was all Jeanie said to Liam, though.

He grinned at that, his rakish look that he knew Jeanie couldn't resist. "I don't doubt that for an instant," said Liam. "I know a bunch of systems designers, if you want some names."

What the fuck was that supposed to mean? That was pretty much a statement that he didn't want to come, wasn't it? *Goddamn.* Jeanie was done with all this bullshit.

"Look, do you want to come or not?" she said. "We both know you're the best systems person in the galaxy."

Liam laughed out loud. "Finally, we can cut all this polite crap," he said. "Would this coming with you include . . . coming with you?"

"Are you asking if I want to stay married?"

"Damned right. I'm tired of the games, babe," said Liam. He sat up on the couch and leaned forward. "I ordered that divorce stuff for you so *you* could cut *me* loose when we got off the pod. That means now. I don't want to leave you, Jeanie. I never did."

"You didn't think I could request the info myself if I wanted it?" said Jeanie, raising her eyebrows at him. Liam's ex hadn't though, not for years.

"And are you going to?" said Liam. "If you don't want me, I'll stay on this depressing little station alone. If you do, I'll join your gang playing hero across the galaxy."

"And you'd be fine with being under my command, on my ship, deferring to me?" said Jeanie.

Liam smiled slowly and licked his lips.

"I've been clear, Li. I want to stay together, as long as you want to be together, and as long as you respect my autonomy."

"Except in the bedroom," said Liam. It wasn't a question. Jeanie's breathing sped up at the look in Liam's eyes.

"Except in the bedroom," she whispered.

"Babe, I'll take orders from you all day as long as you take mine at night," said Liam.

Jeanie rolled her eyes. "Do you hear yourself right now? That's painfully cheesy," said Jeanie, but the thought of it still sent a shiver down her spine.

Liam raised his eyebrows. "So you don't want to, then?" he said, that smile still flitting over his face.

"Shut the fuck up. You know I do," said Jeanie.

"Then," said Liam and held Jeanie's gaze, "tell me what you want." Jeanie couldn't look away and didn't even want to try.

"I want you to pin me down and make me come," said Jeanie. She hadn't even known what she was going to say until the words were already out of her mouth, but it was true.

"Yes," said Liam. "Go and undress and lie in my bunk. I won't leave you waiting long." Liam stood, and Jeanie did the same, turning toward the door to Liam's small cabin. "And Jeanie?" he said, making her stop and turn back. "You may touch yourself if you wish."

Jeanie rolled her eyes again, but the shiver that travelled down her spine was unmistakable. If he was telling her that she was allowed to touch herself, that meant that he could also tell her that she wasn't allowed to . . . Jeanie practically teleported out of her clothes and into Liam's bunk.

He came in just a moment later and held out a blindfold. That wasn't something they had done before. He held it out while his gaze travelled up and down Jeanie's body, making her want to writhe. Liam brandished the blindfold.

"Yes or no?" he said, seriously. Jeanie could say no if she wanted, and Liam would go with it. Part of her wanted to see him, to watch his face, and to know that he could see hers as well, but she couldn't deny the thrill of the blindfold, especially since she had said she wanted him to pin her. To be pinned and not be able to see either, knowing that Liam could do whatever he wanted with her and she wouldn't even know what was coming . . .

"Yes," she whispered.

Liam nodded and quickly slid the blindfold over her eyes. She heard the zipper on Liam's jumpsuit and then the rustle of fabric as he pulled it off. The bunk dipped, and then a light touch trailed down Jeanie's body, between her breasts and across her stomach, and she arched as it travelled down over her hip.

"MS and I had an interesting conversation back on the pod," said Liam.

Jeanie tensed. She'd put safeguards in place so that MS couldn't discuss certain topics, but there was so much that Liam could have gotten out of her regardless. What was he referring to, specifically? Everything she didn't want Liam to find out from her AI came cascading through her mind—

"Come back to me, babe," said Liam, softly. "What's going on?"

"There are just lots of things that I wouldn't want MS to share with you," said Jeanie. "If you find out, I want to tell you myself."

"I didn't ask her about your past, babe," said Liam seriously. "She told me about your relationship with her." Liam trailed his hand up and down her body lightly as he spoke, making it hard for Jeanie to concentrate on his words. "I couldn't understand why you had gone back for her like you did." Liam didn't have to explain when he was talking about. He had been wondering this ever since it happened: Why had she gone back for MS when their moon was imploding instead of coming to find him and make sure he was safe? But he had never come right out and asked her. If he had, she probably would have said that it was because she had faith in him, that he could take care of himself. But with that came the implication that he didn't think the same of her, considering that he had come back for her, and she just didn't want to get into it again. Not to mention that wasn't all of it, though Jeanie couldn't define exactly what the rest of it was.

"What did she tell you?" she said.

"It's simple, actually," said Liam. He walked his fingers down over her hip and trailed them down her thigh, making her twitch. "You made her," he said. "You didn't want your work destroyed."

"That's what she said?" said Jeanie and gasped when he stroked ever so lightly over her clit.

"She said there was a large margin for error," said Liam, dismissively, "but I think she was at least partly right, don't you?" Without warning, Liam pinched and rolled Jeanie's nipple, and she arched and groaned out *yes*, maybe in answer to Liam's question or his actions, likely both.

Liam chuckled. "Seems like talking time is over," he said, "for now." He kept circling her clit as his other hand played over the rest of her. His deep kiss overwhelmed Jeanie's senses and she squirmed as he kissed a warm wet trail down her neck and sucked her nipple into his mouth. He let her come that first time without playing any of their games, and Jeanie felt a little twinge of disappointment. Liam seemed to know though, because he said, "Don't worry, babe, we'll get to that when I have my cock deep inside you." At which she felt down his ribs, his stomach, and his hip. She wrapped her hand around his smooth hardness and gave it a quick stroke, making him groan and shudder before he put his hand over hers. "I seem to recall something about you wanting to be pinned," said Liam. "Thanks for the reminder, babe." He drew one hand over her head, and then the other, keeping his weight on his opposite elbow, and pinned her wrists in one hand. "Is that what you had in mind?" he whispered in her ear.

Jeanie arched and pulled at his grip, revelling in the feel of his hand tightening around her wrists, holding her in place. Her brain was well and truly scrambled at this point; her body seemed to move of its own accord, doing whatever would bring the most pleasure, grinding on him when he moved his hips between her thighs, and then wrapping her legs around him to increase the pressure.

"I thought the point of you being pinned was that you weren't in control," said Liam conversationally.

"The point is I don't have to be," Jeanie ground out. "Fuck me, Li."

"Your wish is my command, babe," said Liam and used his free hand to line himself up and nudge inside.

Jeanie arched again and bucked, trying to draw him in deeper, his hands squeezing tighter around her wrists. Liam groaned and slid in a bit, then set a slow rhythm that had Jeanie growling and writhing, trying to get him to speed up.

"Time to tell me the truth, babe," said Liam, his voice hard now. He whipped the blindfold off her eyes, and Jeanie found herself blinking up into Liam's hard stare. "Do you want me in your new life? Can you truly have your freedom with me there?"

The words hung there between them. Even though Jeanie was the one who could see again, she felt as though Liam removing the blindfold had revealed her innermost workings to him. Liam drove into her hard and then held himself there, grinding his hips against her.

"I'll need an answer from you, babe. Right now."

Liam wasn't sure how long he could hold himself still. He focused on keeping the fear out of his eyes, staying strong for Jeanie. She needed to hear herself say this as much as he needed to hear her say it. The moment stretched on between them until Liam was sure that she was going to say, *No, Li, I can't be free as long as you're there. You'll just tie me down. I'm sorry.* Even thinking those words caused a jolt of fear to shoot up his spine, and he ground himself into Jeanie again.

"I'm still waiting, babe," he growled and moved his face close to her ear, maybe to give himself a moment when he didn't have to look into her eyes. They were swirling with something he couldn't identify, and he didn't know whether he wanted to. "Tell me what you're thinking," he whispered.

Jeanie cleared her throat. "My hip hurts," she said and then flinched. He pulled back to get a look at Jeanie's face, and it turned out her words had shocked her as much as they had him. "Fuck, sorry, Li. I didn't mean to ruin the moment," she said.

Liam took one long breath and quickly gathered his thoughts. She had been honest, she'd said exactly what was on her mind, she'd admitted that she was in pain. That was all good. *Gotta work with this.*

"You haven't ruined anything," he said and pulled out.

"No, I did. That's why you—"

"Ass up, babe," said Liam.

Jeanie gasped and then scrambled to obey him. *God yes.*

"Hands above your head again," he said, "unless you want me to pin your neck?" Her breath caught, but she shook her head.

"No, hands are good," she said and moved them to the bed above her head where he could grasp them again and hold her in place. Liam was going to get as much out of this change in position as he could. He needed to prove to Jeanie that telling him the truth hadn't ruined the moment, that if anything, it had made it better for him, to know that she would tell him if there was a problem and that they could work together to make sure they were in sync. Liam trailed his free hand down Jeanie's side, and around her hip. He gripped the hard ridge of her hipbone, and then lined himself up again, sliding easily inside this time. Her low groan made his hips jerk forward.

"Where were we?" he said, stroking slowly but firmly. He wasn't actually expecting an answer, but it turned out Jeanie managed a semicoherent response.

"You asked me if you being there would ruin my plans," she said.

"And I'm still waiting for your answer, babe," said Liam when she broke off.

"Fuck, no," said Jeanie, and Liam's thoughts swirled. No, it wouldn't ruin her plans, or no, she didn't want him there?

"Care to elaborate?" he said, to give himself a minute. Jeanie was panting now, but she still managed to respond.

"The idea of you following my commands on my ship and then controlling me with orgasms in our cabin is so fucking hot," said Jeanie, and Liam kept his sigh of relief to himself.

"Sure, it's hot with my cock buried deep inside you, but what about the reality?" Liam made himself say it. He had to know for sure. He refused to tie Jeanie down to him if it wasn't what she really wanted.

"Yes," she said, "yes, Li, I've thought about it so many times."

"Thought about it?" said Liam.

"When I thought about my perfect future," whispered Jeanie. Liam shuddered all over and snaked his hand down to press her clit.

"Now you can come all over my cock, babe," he said into her ear, and with a few more thrusts, they came together with Liam's arm wrapped around Jeanie, holding her tight to him.

An endless starscape filled the long outside wall of the empty corridor, floor to ceiling. Jeanie held Liam's hand as they stepped closer, his breathing getting shallow. The planet below them was turning lazily, giving the illusion that they were floating gently around it. Liam seemed very aware that orbiting was less like floating and more like perpetually plummeting toward the planet and barely missing.

Jeanie brushed her fingers over some of the memorials already etched into the window, making them glow softly. Those lost to the void. Liam and Jeanie would probably never be back here; Jeanie's new ship was ready to go, the new crew was waiting for them, and this was their last act before casting off, but it seemed right to put her memorial where she had died.

Jeanie turned to Liam, and he handed her the transfer sheet. She chose a blank corner of the huge window and pressed the sheet into it. It glowed as she peeled it away, leaving a permanent record:

MS1479

You gave your life for ours.

May you and that janky escape pod rest in peace.

Thanks so much for reading *Endless Sea of Stars*! If you liked it, please leave a review on your platform of choice. Even a line or two is very helpful for other readers!

If you want to be the first to hear about new releases, consider joining my newsletter at join.elizabethshearly.ca.

Acknowledgements

Thanks to Chris Baty for helping me to start, and Holly Lisle for helping me to finish.

My most heartfelt thanks to Maggie Morris, The Indie Editor, for her support as the first to read this work and her insights, which greatly improved it.

And, finally, thanks to Chris for keeping a roof over our heads while I chase my dream.

Project Pardus

An entire space station disappears—and someone wants to keep it that way.

All I want is to make a scientific breakthrough that will earn me a legit place in my field. But when I finally nab the perfect project, it's snatched away from me by the granting agency, clearly puppeted by someone powerful.

I refuse to let them bury this, so my ex (the four-armed emotion-sensing alien, Yarrow) and I go after the evidence we need to prove something weird—maybe even sinister—is going on.

When our ship disappears right out from under us, I can no longer risk anyone else for my research...if only everyone would listen when I tell them that. What with folks I meet trying to make friends, and Yarrow following me halfway across the Galaxy, I can't shake off the people who care about me.

Even when I flee my lab. Even when my ship is sabotaged. Even when I shatter space itself.

Also By Elizabeth F. Shearly

Endless Sea Of Stars

Dread Spring

Keep the Good Parts

Project Pardus

Second Acts of Weary Warrior Women

The Swordswoman and the Vampire

To Break A Dragon Bond

A Pentagram Of Candles and Spectres

Her Castle, Her Howl, Her Pack

The King's Pixie Seer

About The Author

Elizabeth F. Shearly writes science fiction and fantasy tales, from flash fiction to novels and everything in between. She holds a B.Sc. in physics, and you'll find plenty of science in her science fiction, though the fiction always takes precedence. No matter what she writes about—spaceships or magic, walking cities or medieval castles—romance always finds a way to blossom, whether as the main plot or as a background story.

When she's not watching characters play-act in her head, you can find her relaxing on the couch with her two cats, playing a video game or knitting a sweater.

patreon.com/ElizabethFShearly

instagram.com/ElizabethFShearly

bookbub.com/authors/elizabeth-f-shearly

facebook.com/ElizabethFShearly/

goodreads.com/elizabethfshearly

pinterest.com/ElizabethFShearly